Orphans

by Lyle Kessler

SAMUEL FRENCH, INC.
45 WEST 25TH STREET	NEW YORK 10010
7623 SUNSET BOULEVARD	HOLLYWOOD 90046
LONDON	*TORONTO*

Date due slip on back cover of book

Special optional music, composed by Pat Metheny and Lyle Mays, which was used in connection with the Off-Broadway New York production, is available *for sale* on either a cassette, at a cost of $21.00, *or* on two reel-to-reel tapes, at a cost of $32.50. Both prices include first-class postage and handling. A cue sheet will be included in all shipments.

AMATEURS: When ordering the above mentioned material, please include the following:

1. Royalty in full for the use of the music ($5.00 music royalty *per performance*) for your entire production.

2. Number of performances and exact performance dates.

STOCK TERMS QUOTED ON APPLICATION TO SAMUEL FRENCH, INC.

ORIGINAL PRODUCTION

Opening Night: August 31, 1983

Matrix Theatre, Los Angeles
Joseph Stern, producer
Actors For Themselves

TREAT ....Paul Lieber
PHILLIP ....Joe Pantoliano
HAROLD..............................Lane Smith

Directed by John Lehne
Scenic design — D. Martyn Bookwalter
Costumes — Doug Spesert
Lighting design — Martin Aronstein
Sound design — Jon Gottlieb
Stage Manager — Kim O'Bannon

STEPPENWOLF THEATRE
COMPANY PRODUCTION

Opening Night: Chicago, February 3, 1985

Artistic Directors ....Terry Kinney and Gary Sinise
Managing Director..................Stephen B. Eich

TREAT...............................Terry Kinney
PHILLIP ....Kevin Anderson
HAROLD..........................John Mahoney

Directed by Gary Sinise
Music — Pat Metheny and Lyle Mays
Sets and Lights — Kevin Rigdon
Costumes — Cookky Gluck
Sound — Gary Sinise and Gregg Winters
Props — Lori S. Sugar
Stage Manager — Douglas Bryan Bean

WESTSIDE ARTS THEATRE

WOLF GANG PRODUCTIONS   **DASHA EPSTEIN**
JOAN CULLMAN   **THE STEPPENWOLF THEATRE COMPANY**

present

THE STEPPENWOLF THEATRE PRODUCTION OF

ORPHANS

by
LYLE KESSLER

Featuring
KEVIN ANDERSON   **TERRY KINNEY**   **JOHN MAHONEY**

Music by
PAT METHENY & LYLE MAYS

Set and Lighting by	*Sound*	*Sound Supervising*
KEVIN RIGDON	**GARY SINISE**	**CHUCK LONDON MEDIA/ STEWART WERNER**

Costumes by	*Property Designer*	*Stage Manager/ Asst. Lighting Designer*
COOKIE GLUCK	**LORI S. SUGAR**	**DOUGLAS BRYAN BEAN**

Directed by
GARY SINISE

Original production of **ORPHANS** by Actors for Themselves at the Matrix Theatre,
Los Angeles, California, Joseph Stern, Artistic Director.

CAST
(in order of appearance)

Phillip .... **KEVIN ANDERSON**
Treat .... **TERRY KINNEY**
Harold .... **JOHN MAHONEY**

The action takes place in an old row house in North Philadelphia.

ACT I
A spring day.

ACT II
Two weeks later.

THERE WILL BE ONE FIFTEEN-MINUTE INTERMISSION.

UNDERSTUDIES

Understudies never substitute for listed players unless a specific announcement
for their appearance is made at the time of the performance.
For Phillip, Treat—**Christopher Fields;** for Harold—**William Wise.**

MUSICAL CREDITS
In Order

Songs	*Album*
"Phase Dance" **	Pat Metheny Group
"Bright Size Life" *	Bright Size Life
"Are You Going With Me?" **	Off Ramp
"Tell It All" **	First Circle
"Hermitage" *	New Chatauqua
"Eighteen" ***	Off Ramp
"If I Could" *	First Circle
"First Circle" **	First Circle
"Jaco" *	Pat Metheny Group
"Sueno Con Mexico" *	New Chatauqua
"Au Lait" **	Off Ramp
"Barcarole" ***	Off Ramp
"Long Ago Child" *	New Chautauqua
"Farmer's Trust" *	Travels
"Oasis" *	Watercolors

*Pat Metheny
**Pat Metheny and Lyle Mays
***Pat Metheny, Lyle Mays, and Nina Vasconselos

Orphans

ACT ONE

SCENE 1

*North Philadelphia. An old row house. A cluttered liv-
ing room. A closet. A TV set on the floor. A worn
frayed couch with a couple of books and a newspaper on it. A small table with a large empty bottle
of Hellman's mayonnaise. A couple of old chairs. A
large window with a window seat by the front door.
On the other side of the living room another smaller
window above a pantry area leading to the kitchen.
On the pantry shelf is a stack of Star Kist tuna cans.*
PHILLIP *is silhouetted in the window seat, blowing bub-
bles. Above him on the window ledge, is a woman's
red shoe. The room is in semi-darkness.* PHILLIP
*looks out the window and sees something. He jumps
up, runs across the room, stuffs the books on the
couch under the cushions, grabs the newspaper,
shuts off the TV, puts the paper by the window seat,
starts upstairs, turns back, rushes to the window,
grabs the red shoe and shoves it inside the window
seat. He runs upstairs.*
*The front door opens and slams shut. The lights come
up full.* TREAT, *back against the door, catches his
breath. He looks out the window and is satisfied,
relaxes, snaps his fingers and enters the room, looking around. He crosses to the table, picks up the
empty mayonnaise bottle and shakes his head. He
pulls a piece of jewelry from his jacket pocket and
drops it on the table.*

TREAT. (*calling*) Phillip? Phillip? (*yells*) Phillip, you

hear me! (*He continues to empty his pockets of brace-lets and jewelry.*) You home, Phillip! I imagine you're home! Where the hell else you gonna be, huh! I imagine you're hiding from your big brother Treat! (*He starts to study the jewelry.*) Come on out, Phillip! I ain't in the mood for no hide-and-go-seek game. You hear me! Come on the fuck out!

(*PHILLIP appears from upstairs.*)

PHILLIP. Don't tag me.

TREAT. I ain't gonna tag you.

PHILLIP. 'Cause I'm sick and tired of being *it*, Treat.

TREAT. I ain't gonna tag you. I told you. I ain't play-ing no games.

PHILLIP. You said that yesterday.

TREAT. Yesterday's yesterday. Today's today.

PHILLIP. You promise?

TREAT. I promise. How long you been hiding?

PHILLIP. I don't know.

TREAT. Half the day, I bet.

PHILLIP. I didn't keep count.

TREAT. You eat lunch?

PHILLIP. Uh huh.

TREAT. What you have?

PHILLIP. I had Star Kist tuna.

TREAT. Mayonnaise?

PHILLIP. Uh huh. Hellman's.

TREAT. How much mayonnaise you have?

PHILLIP. Couple of tablespoons.

TREAT. If you only had a couple of tablespoons, how come we're out of it?

PHILLIP. Hellman's goes fast, Treat.

TREAT. It goes fast, all right. A half a bottle a day. (*TREAT tags PHILLIP suddenly.*) You're it, Phillip.

PHILLIP. No!

TREAT. You're fucking it!

PHILLIP. You promised.

TREAT. I had my fingers crossed.

PHILLIP. I come out 'cause you said you wouldn't.
(*PHILLIP chases TREAT around the room. He catches him and tags him.*)

TREAT. Time out!

PHILLIP. No!

TREAT. Fucking time out, Phillip. The game's over.
(*PHILLIP throws himself down on the couch, sulking.*)
Where were you?

PHILLIP. I ain't telling.

TREAT. Come on.

PHILLIP. No, it's my secret.

TREAT. I know where you been anyway.

PHILLIP. Where?

TREAT. In the closet.

PHILLIP. How you know that?

TREAT. It's your favorite hiding place.

PHILLIP. I was hiding in there waiting for you to come home.

TREAT. Just standing and waiting, huh?

PHILLIP. Uh huh.

TREAT. Just standing and hiding in the darkness, waiting for your big brother Treat to come home.

PHILLIP. I like it in there. It's warm.

TREAT. I wouldn't know.

PHILLIP. It's got all of Mom's coats in there.

TREAT. We ought to get rid of them.

PHILLIP. No!

TREAT. What good they doing hanging there all these years?

PHILLIP. I want them.

TREAT. They ain't doing nobody any good.

PHILLIP. They're not bothering anybody, Treat. They're just hanging there.

TREAT. People find out about you, they're gonna put you away.

PHILLIP. They won't put me away!

TREAT. A grown man standing all day in a dark closet.

PHILLIP. I done other things.

TREAT. What other things you do?

PHILLIP. I looked out the window.

TREAT. Good.

PHILLIP. I seen some things.

TREAT. What you see?

PHILLIP. I seen a man and a dog, a man walking a big black dog. (*imitates the dog*)

TREAT. What else?

PHILLIP. I seen a woman walking like this. (*demonstrates, swishing from side to side*) Seen another woman, a tiny, tiny woman. (*demonstrates tiny steps*)

TREAT. Anything else?

PHILLIP. Plenty else.

TREAT. Go on.

PHILLIP. A man with two big boys, man in the middle, boys on each side.

TREAT. What were they doing?

PHILLIP. Goin' swimming maybe, goin' to the movies, probably. Gonna see John Wayne in "The Halls of Montezuma."

TREAT. You got an imagination.

PHILLIP. I seen other things. I seen a man with a woman, man walking arm and arm with a woman. (*demonstrates*) Woman had long red hair.

TREAT. Long red hair, huh. Was the man balding?

PHILLIP. Man was balding, right.

TREAT. Woman had bangles dangling from her wrist, woman loaded with bangles, am I right?

PHILLIP. You're right, Treat.

TREAT. I see that couple. (*TREAT picks up a piece of jewelry from the table and shows him.*) What else you do!

PHILLIP. I watched TV.

TREAT. What did you watch?

PHILLIP. I watched reruns. I watched "The Price is Right."

TREAT. That's a woman's show!

PHILLIP. They have fabulous prizes, Treat.

TREAT. You'd like to win one, I bet.

PHILLIP. They won a hi-fi stereo combination, a year's supply of l.p.'s and cassettes; they won a mahogany dining room set, they won an Electro Lux golf cart and a Bendix freezer filled with five hundred filet mignons.

TREAT. You remember all that.

PHILLIP. They won a year's subscription to National Geographic. They won a . . .

TREAT. That's enough!

PHILLIP. I'd like to get that National Geographic.

TREAT. What would you do with it?

PHILLIP. I'd look at it.

TREAT. You'd read it?

PHILLIP. You know I couldn't read it, Treat. I'd look at the pictures, though. They got real nice pictures, pictures of all kinds of animals and primitive tribes.

TREAT. I bumped into that woman and man today. Man was balding, woman had long red hair.

PHILLIP. That's right.

TREAT. I had a real good day today, Phillip. I'm gonna go out, tonight, gonna celebrate!

PHILLIP. We all outta mayonnaise, Treat. You go out,

will you bring home an extra large bottle of Hellman's mayonnaise?

TREAT. Yes sirree, had a hell of a day, Phillip. You interested? (*TREAT gathers up jewelry, wallets, rings, and puts them away in a dresser drawer.*)

PHILLIP. I'm interested, Treat. Only thing is I got a real taste in my mouth for that Hellman's.

TREAT. (*picks up more jewelry*) Guy wasn't carrying much, just a few bucks, but he had a real nice wrist watch. Wadaya think?

PHILLIP. It's nice.

TREAT. Man had good taste, woman didn't have bad taste either. Look at this! (*a woman's wrist watch*) Tiny little wrists, tiny little dainty little wrists.

PHILLIP. She wore this?

TREAT. No more. Bumped into another fellow earlier today, Fairmount Park. Fellow put up a struggle.

PHILLIP. No kidding.

TREAT. I said, "What you gettin' violent about, Mister, no point in gettin' violent!"

PHILLIP. What did he say?

TREAT. He kicked at me.

PHILLIP. He kicked you?

TREAT. Right in the shin.

PHILLIP. Let's see.

TREAT. (*rolling up his pants*) See. Gonna be fucking black and blue.

PHILLIP. I'll get the Hydrogen Peroxide. (*He goes off.*)

TREAT. You remember all them brand names.

PHILLIP. (*off*) Uh huh.

TREAT. How come you can do that?

PHILLIP. (*returns with bottle*) I don't know.

TREAT. I mean you don't have much of an intellect for

anything else, but you know them brand names and the names of all them various prizes.

PHILLIP. It just comes to me.

TREAT. I said, "Listen, Mister, I don't appreciate getting kicked in the shins like that."

PHILLIP. What did he do?

TREAT. He cursed at me.

PHILLIP. He cursed you?

TREAT. All kinds of names, names I wouldn't even repeat. Terrible fucking filth came out of that man's mouth.

PHILLIP. What did he look like?

TREAT. Dressed real nice, had on a suit and tie. Must have driven over to Fairmount Park. It was a real nice spring day, today, Phillip. Too bad you can't go out and enjoy it. Man figured he'd take a little walk in Fairmount Park.

PHILLIP. What happened?

TREAT. Had a lot of money on him, that's why he put up a struggle, I guess, must've had three, four hundred dollars.

PHILLIP. Where is he?

TREAT. Left him there, had to cut him though. Not bad, just superficial. Warned him! In fact, said, "Mister, you're gettin' me pissed off kickin' me like that."

PHILLIP. Did you show him the bruise?

TREAT. I didn't have to show him the bruise. Got me pissed off. I had to take out my knife, had to cut him. (*TREAT takes a switchblade out, and demonstrates.*)

PHILLIP. Did he bleed?

TREAT. Just a little bit, Phillip. It's amazing, how people stop struggling once there's a little blood. (*sticks switchblade into the table*) Paper come?

PHILLIP. Uh huh.

TREAT. Let's have it.

PHILLIP. Come early this morning. (*hands it to TREAT*)

TREAT. What's this, Phillip?

PHILLIP. What's what?

TREAT. How come this word is underlined?

PHILLIP. I don't know.

TREAT. (*scanning paper*) How come there are underlined words in this here Philadelphia Inquirer!

PHILLIP. I have no idea, Treat.

TREAT. Here's a word, dispensation. You underline this word?

PHILLIP. I didn't touch that word.

TREAT. You read this word?

PHILLIP. No.

TREAT. You got a dictionary, Phillip?

PHILLIP. I got no dictionary.

TREAT. (*stalking him*) You sure you don't have no pocket dictionary somewhere in this house? You sure you ain't spending the day reading the newspaper and books, underlining words, looking up the meaning of particular words, getting yourself an education?

PHILLIP. (*running from him*) I got no education!

TREAT. You know the alphabet?

PHILLIP. No!

TREAT. I bet you know the fuckin' alphabet. I bet you're holding out on me.

PHILLIP. I ain't holding out on you, Treat.

TREAT. What's this word mean, what's this fuckin' dispensation mean?

PHILLIP. I don't know, Treat.

TREAT. Who underlined this fuckin' dispensation!

PHILLIP. It wasn't me!

TREAT. Someone come in the house while I was away?

PHILLIP. I don't know.

TREAT. You would have heard him.

PHILLIP. I was in the closet.

TREAT. Someone steal in the house while you were standing in the closet and underline this word?

PHILLIP. Maybe.

TREAT. Where is he?

PHILLIP. I don't know.

TREAT. Is he still here?

PHILLIP. He might be.

TREAT. Find him.

PHILLIP. All right.

TREAT. Kill him! (*hands PHILLIP the knife*) I want him dead, you understand! Man stealing in my house like that. (*PHILLIP runs around the room looking everywhere.*)

PHILLIP. Maybe he's upstairs.

TREAT. Yea, maybe.

PHILLIP. Maybe he's hiding under the bed.

TREAT. I wouldn't put it past him, hiding under the bed, waiting for us to go to sleep.

PHILLIP. I'll get him!

(*PHILLIP goes upstairs. TREAT sits on the couch. The sound of a crash is heard from upstairs. TREAT doesn't move. More noise.*)

PHILLIP. (*off*) SON OF A BITCH! (*PHILLIP comes downstairs holding his arm.*) That son of a bitch!

TREAT. You get him?

PHILLIP. No Treat, he got me.

TREAT. Wadaya mean?

PHILLIP. I'm bleeding. I was looking under the bed and he came out of the closet.

TREAT. Let's see. (*PHILLIP shows his arm to TREAT.*) That ain't bad. That's just a scratch.

PHILLIP. I jumped back and banged into the night table. The lamp fell over.

TREAT. I heard it.

PHILLIP. If I hadn't jumped back he would have stabbed me right through the back, Treat.

TREAT. Lucky for you. Where is he?

PHILLIP. He leaped out the window.

TREAT. He got away?

PHILLIP. Yes.

TREAT. What did he look like?

PHILLIP. Errol Flynn.

TREAT. Errol Flynn?

PHILLIP. The movie actor.

TREAT. I know Errol Flynn!

PHILLIP. He could've broke a leg leaping outta the window like that, Treat. He must be some kind of athlete.

TREAT. Maybe I better put on some hydrogen peroxide.

PHILLIP. No, Treat, it burns.

TREAT. You don't want it to get infected. (*TREAT gets the hydrogen peroxide.*)

PHILLIP. It's not gonna get infected.

TREAT. You don't wanna lose your arm. (*holds the hydrogen peroxide*)

PHILLIP. I ain't gonna lose my arm.

TREAT. Come here, Phillip. Let me help you. Let your big brother Treat take care of you. (*TREAT stands holding the bottle of hydrogen peroxide. PHILLIP slowly walks towards him.*)

SCENE 2

*That night. Late. TREAT and HAROLD can be heard
   outside.*

HAROLD. (*off, singing*)
"If I had the wings of an angel,
Over these prison walls I would fly."
   TREAT. (*off*) Right this way, Harold. We're home.
   HAROLD. (*off, singing*)
"Straight to the arms of me mutter,
And there I'd be willing to die."

(*TREAT and HAROLD enter. HAROLD is drunk. He
   is a middle-aged man wearing an expensive suit and
   carrying a briefcase.*)

HAROLD. You know that song, Treat? You remember
that song?
   TREAT. I can't say I do.
   HAROLD. You're not a Dead End Kid, are you?
   TREAT. A Dead End Kid?
   HAROLD. 'Cause if you were a Dead End Kid I'd give
you everything I had . . . I swear to God . . . I'd give you
the very shirt off my back.
   TREAT. You don't have to go that far.
   HAROLD. There are no limits as far as the Dead End
Kids and me are concerned.
   TREAT. No kidding.
   HAROLD. I love those fucking Dead End Kids.
   TREAT. I'm no Dead End Kid, Harold.
   HAROLD. What a shame.
   TREAT. You wanna drink?

HAROLD. Don't mind if I do.

TREAT. You like it straight?

HAROLD. Straight as an arrow.

TREAT. Coming up!

HAROLD. I'm from Chicago, you know, born and bred. (*TREAT hides the briefcase.*)

TREAT. You told me.

HAROLD. Grew up in an orphanage, didn't have no mommy or daddy, just had them Dead End Kids.

TREAT. I never seen 'em.

HAROLD. You never seen them on late night TV?

TREAT. No.

HAROLD. All them Dead End Kids running around that 12-inch screen, all them itty bitty Dead End Kids on an itty bitty 12-inch screen.

TREAT. No, I haven't.

HAROLD. It's not the same as seeing them on a big wide motion picture screen. How can you enjoy little itty bitty Dead End Kids no bigger than the fingers on your hand.

TREAT. I guess you can't.

HAROLD. They had a little Irish mother, though. *Top of the morning* Irish mother . . . I loved that woman. Corn beef and cabbage cooking night and day. I used to work up a hearty appetite just sitting in them dark Chicago movie houses watching those Dead End Kids. (*sniffs the air*) Anything cooking in this house?

TREAT. Nothing cooking right now, Harold.

HAROLD. How come?

TREAT. It's 2 A.M.

HAROLD. That's what I'm saying . . . If you were to walk into that Dead End Kid's house, any time day or night, Dead End Kid's house smelling of corn beef and cabbage, why you just walk straight into the kitchen and cut yourself a piece. Jesus Christ, Treat, my mouth is watering, my fucking mouth is watering!

TREAT. You want something to eat?

HAROLD. I'm starving to death.

TREAT. There's tuna.

HAROLD. Tuna.

TREAT. Star Kist tuna.

HAROLD. (*looking around*) Where the fuck am I?

TREAT. You're in my house.

HAROLD. You're offering me tuna!

TREAT. Uh huh.

HAROLD. Fucking tuna! Where's my briefcase?

TREAT. Over here.

HAROLD. Let's have it.

TREAT. I was watching it for you.

HAROLD. I can do my own watching. Let's have it. (*TREAT hands him the briefcase. HAROLD starts to walk to the door.*)

TREAT. Where you going?

HAROLD. I'm leaving. (*TREAT trips HAROLD, who falls to the floor.*)

TREAT. You can't walk.

HAROLD. (*on floor*) I can't walk, can I?

TREAT. You're not in any shape.

HAROLD. How did this happen?

TREAT. You were drinking.

HAROLD. It's not like me.

TREAT. You're pissed!

HAROLD. How 'bout that!

TREAT. You're lying on the floor pissed, Harold.

HAROLD. It must be because I met a Dead End Kid after all these years, I finally met a fucking Dead End Kid.

TREAT. I'm no Dead End Kid.

HAROLD. Don't kid me. (*He crawls to the foot of the couch, dragging his briefcase.*)

TREAT. I ain't kidding you.

HAROLD. I know a Dead End Kid when I see one.

TREAT. You don't smell no corn beef and cabbage around here! (*HAROLD leans against the couch, cradling the briefcase, and picks up his drink.*)

HAROLD. Don't matter! No corn beef and cabbage cooking where I come from either . . . come from an orphanage, goddamn orphanage, no Irish top-of-the-morning mother there either, just a big son-of-a-bitching German, wore a chef's hat and a filthy dirty apron. German slept right in the kitchen. Orphans always hungry, orphans love to come down in the middle of the night and raid the refrigerator. German slept there, one eye open, break your back if he caught you, break every bone in your body. Took a liking to me though, filled my plate with meat and potatoes, lucky for me, orphans always coughing up blood, orphans dropping dead all the time, terrible mortality rate at an orphanage! . . . Thank god for them big heaping plates of meat and potatoes . . . thank god for that bloody fucking German son of a bitch. (*HAROLD is falling asleep. TREAT moves in to get the briefcase. HAROLD wakes.*) You know what orphans call out in the middle of the night, Treat?

TREAT. (*moves back*) No, what do they call out, Harold? (*PHILLIP peeks down the stairs.*)

HAROLD. Motherless orphans, middle of the night Chicago, orphans on a big hill facing Lake Michigan. Wind come through there making a terrible sound, wind come through there going Hissssss! Orphans pulling their blankets up over their heads, frightened orphans crying out. You know what they were crying?

TREAT. No.

HAROLD. *Mommy! Mommy!* Honest to god! Mother-less orphans don't know a mommy from a daddy, don't know a mommy from a fuckin' tangerine . . . poor motherless bastards, calling *Mommy . . . Mommy . . .*

TREAT. Harold?

HAROLD. *Mommy . . . (Quiet. HAROLD is asleep on the floor. TREAT takes HAROLD's briefcase to the table. PHILLIP moves slowly down the stairs.)*

TREAT. Woke you up, huh?

PHILLIP. Who is he, Treat?

TREAT. Name's Harold.

PHILLIP. He's an orphan.

TREAT. You were listening.

PHILLIP. He's from Chicago, had a real bad child-hood.

TREAT. That's what he said.

PHILLIP. Where'd you find him, Treat? (*TREAT removes HAROLD's wallet.*)

TREAT. Downtown Philly, haven't hung out there for a while. Man was drinking alone, thought he recognized me, thought I was a Dead End Kid.

HAROLD. Mommy . . .

PHILLIP. A Dead End Kid?

TREAT. Can you imagine? He was pie-eyed, thought I was a fuckin' Dead End Kid.

PHILLIP. I seen 'em on TV.

TREAT. You and he have a lot in common.

PHILLIP. Can he stay for a while?

TREAT. He'll stay all right. (*holds up papers from briefcase*) Look at this, Phillip. Know what this is?

PHILLIP. What?

TREAT. Stocks and bonds. Man's walking around with a million bucks worth of securities under his arm. We hit paydirt this time. Dumb son of a bitch. He could have passed out. Somebody could have mugged him.

PHILLIP. Somebody could have kidnapped him.

TREAT. That's right! Kidnapped him and held him for ransom. Bet you could get a million bucks for a guy like this, maybe even two million. (*He is on the floor next to HAROLD, tries to lift him under his arms, can't . . .*) Guy's probably an industrialist, probably be on the front page of the Philadelphia Inquirer in a day or two, so and so, industrialist, missing.

PHILLIP. You think so?

TREAT. Look at his shoes. Genuine alligator.

PHILLIP. He's got a real nice suit.

TREAT. It's silk. (*TREAT is still trying.*)

PHILLIP. (*touching the jacket material*) I like the way it feels, Treat.

TREAT. It's genuine silk, Phillip. Man's worth a fortune. (*exasperated*) Get his feet! (*They carry him to one of the wooden chairs. TREAT finds a small piece of rope.*) I need more rope!

PHILLIP. Rope!

(*PHILLIP exits to the kitchen. TREAT ties HAROLD's feet. A loud noise from the kitchen. It grows louder. TREAT stops and listens. A terrible racket.*)

PHILLIP. (*off*) I can't find it.

TREAT. It's under the fuckin' sink, Phillip.

PHILLIP. I found it. (*PHILLIP enters with a long rope that trails into the kitchen. TREAT pulls on it. He ties HAROLD's hands behind the chair. He wraps rope around his chest and the chair.*) I like his face, Treat.

TREAT. Don't get attached to it.

PHILLIP. He's got a friendly face.

TREAT. There's no point in getting attached to it.

PHILLIP. What are you gonna do with him?

TREAT. I haven't decided.

PHILLIP. You're not gonna cut him, are you?

TREAT. That depends.

HAROLD. (*in his sleep*)
"If I had the wings of an angel,
Over these prison walls I would fly . . ."

PHILLIP. What's he singing?

TREAT. (*finishes tying him*) He's singing a song.

HAROLD. "Straight to the arms of me mutter . . ."

TREAT. I need some tape. (*TREAT crosses to the window seat. HAROLD mumbles in his sleep.*)

HAROLD. Ahhh ya mutter.

PHILLIP. (*repeating*) Ahhh ya mutter!

HAROLD. Ahhh ya crumb.

PHILLIP. (*repeating*) Ahhh ya crumb!

HAROLD. (*mumbling*) Da mark of da squealer. (*TREAT at the window seat pulls out a very high high-heeled woman's red shoe.*)

TREAT. What's this, Phillip?

PHILLIP. I found it.

TREAT. Wadaya mean?

PHILLIP. I cleaned under the sofa, Treat. I moved it.

TREAT. Who told you to move the sofa?

PHILLIP. I never cleaned under there before. I felt it was time.

TREAT. Where's the other?

PHILLIP. There's no other.

TREAT. There's only one?

PHILLIP. Uh huh.

TREAT. Woman have only one foot?

PHILLIP. I don't think so, Treat. I think she must have two feet, only she lost one of her shoes.

TREAT. You figured that out?

PHILLIP. Yes.

TREAT. You figured that out all by yourself, huh? You must be doing a lot of figuring.

PHILLIP. (*moves away*) I haven't been doing any figuring, Treat.

TREAT. The way I see it, woman has only one foot! (*backs him to couch*) Maybe you're pulling my chain, Phillip. Maybe you ain't hanging out in no closet all the day.

PHILLIP. I ain't pulling your chain, Treat.

TREAT. Maybe you're seeing all kinds of people while I'm out working, making us a living. Maybe you were looking out the window and this real nice looking lady walked by on these very high high-heeled shoes. You sure you didn't tap on this window, Phillip, and motion her in?

PHILLIP. (*tries to get away*) I never tapped on no window.

TREAT. You sure you didn't undress her on this here very sofa? You sure the two of you didn't have an afternoon of it here on our sofa and she had to leave in a hurry, running out holding her one shoe?

PHILLIP. That never happened.

TREAT. I want this shoe out of here. (*He throws the shoe on the couch next to PHILLIP, crosses to the window seat and removes the tape.*)

PHILLIP. Maybe it was Mom's shoe, Treat. Maybe it's been there all these years.

TREAT. This ain't Mom's shoe. Mom never would have worn a shoe like this.

PHILLIP. What was she like, Treat?

TREAT. I don't remember. I was a kid at the time. You was a baby.

PHILLIP. I remember her hand, Treat. I remember her holding my hand. It felt real nice and warm. (*TREAT crosses to HAROLD, tightens his ropes. PHILLIP crosses to TREAT, touches him on the shoulder. TREAT, startled, jumps back.*) Can I keep it?

TREAT. No, get it out.

PHILLIP. I wanna keep it.

TREAT. I'm gonna lose my temper. (*PHILLIP hands the shoe to TREAT.*)

PHILLIP. I can't see why I can't keep it, Treat. I'll put it in my room, outta sight. It'll never bother you again.

TREAT. I don't want it in your room. I don't want it in this house!

PHILLIP. All right.

TREAT. Open the window!

PHILLIP. What for?

TREAT. Open it! (*PHILLIP wraps a scarf around his face. He opens the window. TREAT throws the shoe out on the lawn. He closes the window. PHILLIP looks out.*)

PHILLIP. It's on the lawn.

TREAT. It's outta here.

PHILLIP. It's just sitting on the lawn.

TREAT. Forget it.

HAROLD. (*sleeping*) Mommy! Mommy!

PHILLIP. What's he doing?

TREAT. He's having a bad dream. (*stuffs HAROLD's mouth with a hanky and tapes his mouth*) Go to bed, Phillip. Get some sleep. You have a big day tomorrow. You're gonna have to keep Harold company. I'm gonna be downtown, making some inquiries. We hit paydirt, Phillip. We're gonna be fuckin' rich!

Scene 3

The next day. HAROLD tied up in the chair, tape covering his mouth. PHILLIP is at the window, looking out.

PHILLIP. Here comes somebody! Here comes an old man with a cane, got a newspaper under his arm, a little brown bag . . . probably has some Squibb's Mineral Oil in that brown bag, maybe a jar of Planter's Peanut Butter and a loaf of Friehoffer's Bakery bread. Gonna make himself some nice thick peanut butter sandwiches.

HAROLD. Mmmmm.

PHILLIP. You say something, Mister?

HAROLD. Mmmmm.

PHILLIP. You speaking to me?

HAROLD. Mmmmm.

PHILLIP. You hungry? Maybe you're hungry, maybe that's it. You working up an appetite listening to me talk about those delicious peanut butter sandwiches that old man is gonna make?

HAROLD. Mmmmmm.

PHILLIP. (*crosses to HAROLD*) Treat's gonna be home real soon now. Probably make you a tuna sandwich, Star Kist tuna and mayo on toast. How's that sound?

HAROLD. (*turns away*) Mmmmmm.

PHILLIP. Mmmmm. I figured you'd like that. I've been eating Star Kist tuna for lunch for years now. I used to make myself peanut butter sandwiches, but I got sick of them. I like variety in my food. (*at window*) Look at that, Mister! Two girls walking by . . . you're really missing something. (*runs across room to other window*) One's wearing real tight dungarees, the other's got on a skirt. I like the one with them tight dungarees. Only thing is Mister, there's a shoe out there now, a shoe staring me straight in the face, driving me crazy. (*crosses to HAROLD*) Listen Mister, if I climb out this window and bring back that shoe, you'll keep it to yourself, won't you?

HAROLD. Mmmmmm.

PHILLIP. 'Cause Treat has a hell of a temper, especially if he's crossed. He was in and out of the House of Detention when he was a kid. Him and me are brothers! (*runs to window, stops, turns, crosses to couch*) Only thing is I ain't supposed to go out Mister, 'cause I have a terrible allergy, allergic to most everything: plants, grass, trees, pollen. I almost died once! I went on over to Linton's restaurant, corner of Broad and Olney, with Treat . . . my face got red, tongue swelled up, I was gasping for breath. I got it, Mister! I'll hold my breath so's I don't breathe in any of that deadly pollen. (*runs to window, turns*) I can trust you, can't I Mister? You're gonna keep your mouth shut, ain't you?

HAROLD. Mmmmmm.

PHILLIP. Okay. (*PHILLIP takes a deep breath, wraps the scarf around his face, opens the window and climbs out. As soon as he is out, HAROLD rocks back and forth and stands with the chair tied to him. He hops to the other side of the couch and sits down. PHILLIP climbs in the window with the shoe. He closes the window, unwraps the scarf, and takes a deep breath. He turns and sees HAROLD. Upset:*) What are you doing over there, Mister?

HAROLD. Mmmmmm.

PHILLIP. How did you get over there?

HAROLD. Mmmmmm.

PHILLIP. You shouldn't be over there.

HAROLD. Mmmmmm.

PHILLIP. I don't think Treat is gonna like this. You're supposed to be sitting over here.

HAROLD. Mmmmmm.

PHILLIP. Only thing is, I ain't supposed to touch you, I'm only supposed to watch you and see that everything is okay. I don't know what I'm gonna do now, Mister. Treat's gonna come home soon and ask how come you're over there, and I don't know what I'm gonna say.

HAROLD. Mmmmm.

PHILLIP. What are you saying?

HAROLD. Mmmmmm!

PHILLIP. I don't know what you're saying.

HAROLD. (*through gag*) Take the fuckin' gag off!

PHILLIP. I can't take off your gag, 'cause I ain't supposed to touch you. (*PHILLIP runs across to the pantry window and looks out.*) Treat's gonna be pissed off when he gets back. He's gonna kick my ass. He's gonna say how come you ain't doin' what I say, Phillip, how come you ain't watchin' him! (*HAROLD bends his head behind a cushion at the back of the couch. He comes up with the tape missing. PHILLIP turns around and sees him.*) How'd you do that, Mister!

HAROLD. (*smiling, simply*) I'm an admirer of Houdini's, real name was Erich Weiss. Yiddisha boy, Houdini, don't let the Italian flavor fool you, born Erich Weiss, east side of New York.

PHILLIP. What am I gonna say to Treat?

HAROLD. Let me take care of that.

PHILLIP. He's gonna slap me around.

HAROLD. He's not going to touch you.

PHILLIP. He's not?

HAROLD. You think I would let him touch you!

PHILLIP. You wouldn't?

HAROLD. He's not going to lay a hand on you.

PHILLIP. How can you stop him?

HAROLD. I have my ways.

PHILLIP. Treat's got a violent temper.

HAROLD. I love violent tempers.

PHILLIP. He see you over there he's gonna go crazy.

HAROLD. I'm not going to be over here.

PHILLIP. (*startled*) Where you gonna be!

HAROLD. I'm going to be sitting on the couch probably, sitting reading the Philadelphia Inquirer.

PHILLIP. You are?

HAROLD. Uh huh. You have the Inquirer?

PHILLIP. Yes.

HAROLD. I'm going to be reading the Financial section probably, or maybe even the Sports section, depends on when he comes home. What's your name?

PHILLIP. Phillip.

HAROLD. Phillip, mine's Harold. Please to meet you. (*HAROLD stands tied to the chair, wiggles his fingers.*)

PHILLIP. I better not.

HAROLD. You don't want to shake?

PHILLIP. Treat said not to touch you.

HAROLD. Not ever?

PHILLIP. I don't know.

HAROLD. Or did he mean just now, just today?

PHILLIP. I didn't ask him.

HAROLD. Because that would be a shame if we could never touch. I mean, if I could never put my arm around your shoulders and give them an encouraging squeeze. How come you walk around with your shoes untied?

PHILLIP. I don't know how to lace 'em.

HAROLD. You don't know how to tie a knot?

PHILLIP. I try, but they get all tangled up. They get impossible to unknot.

HAROLD. That's no crime. Man doesn't have to know how to tie a knot. Didn't you ever hear of loafers?

PHILLIP. Loafers?

HAROLD. You have no need of laces with loafers. Didn't anyone ever tell you that?

PHILLIP. No.

HAROLD. You're a deprived person, Phillip. Here I am talking to a deprived person. You don't know the principle behind electricity, do you?

PHILLIP. No.

HAROLD. But you can turn on a light. Don't need to learn how to tie laces either, wear loafers instead. No one'll know the difference. What color you like?

PHILLIP. Wadaya mean?

HAROLD. What color loafer?

PHILLIP. I don't know. Green?

HAROLD. Green's no good. Don't go with your personality. What about pale yellow?

PHILLIP. Pale yellow's okay.

HAROLD. I'm going to buy you a pair of pale yellow loafers.

PHILLIP. You are?

HAROLD. That's not the half of it, going to buy you a lot of things, going to buy you a whole new wardrobe, make you presentable, going to teach you how to behave in company.

PHILLIP. I don't know how to behave.

HAROLD. You'll learn. Going to teach you etiquette, teach you the proper way to cut your meat, knife in the right hand, not in the left. Fuck laces, you're going to be wearing loafers from now on in. This is a real tragic situation I've wandered into, one boy's a delinquent, in and out of the House of Detention, the other's boy's shoulders just dying for a gentle encouraging squeeze.

PHILLIP. They are?

HAROLD. Anybody ever give your shoulders an encouraging squeeze?

PHILLIP. I don't think so.

HAROLD. That's a tragedy. Every young man's shoulders need an encouraging squeeze now and then.

PHILLIP. Treat never did that.

HAROLD. I imagine not. What about your father?

PHILLIP. I don't know. He ran away from home when I was small.

HAROLD. He deserted the family?

PHILLIP. Yes.

HAROLD. Well, I know shoulders, Phillip. If I know anything, I know about shoulders. (*His arm comes out, free.*) You want me to give them a squeeze, try it out, see how it feels?

PHILLIP. (*hesitantly*) I don't know.

HAROLD. You don't have to touch me. I'll touch you.

PHILLIP. Well, maybe that would be all right.

HAROLD. That would be fine. Come on over here. Come on. (*puts his arm around PHILLIP's shoulders, long pause*) How's that feel?

PHILLIP. Feels okay.

HAROLD. Feels good?

PHILLIP. Yes.

HAROLD. Feels real good?

PHILLIP. Yes, feels real good.

HAROLD. Feels encouraging, huh?

PHILLIP. Uh huh.

HAROLD. Makes you feel there's hope.

PHILLIP. Yes.

HAROLD. (*squeezing*) This is what you missed.

PHILLIP. Yes.

HAROLD. That feeling.

PHILLIP. I missed that.

HAROLD. You got it now.

PHILLIP. I do?

HAROLD. Forever and ever, Phillip. I would never leave you.

PHILLIP. You wouldn't?

HAROLD. No.

PHILLIP. What will Treat say?

HAROLD. Treat doesn't have anything to do with it.

PHILLIP. He might not like it.

HAROLD. Let me worry about Treat. You got an intellect, you know that, Phillip.

PHILLIP. I do?

HAROLD. Positively. Don't let anyone tell you any different. Never came out, that's all, you never let it out. (*HAROLD wriggles out of the rest of the ropes.*)

PHILLIP. You're getting out!

HAROLD. I'm no Houdini, though. I mean, you put me in chains or a straight jacket, I'd have a hell of a time. Imagine that jewboy getting out of all them contraptions, son of a gun jewboy, Erich Weiss, he had a nerve, didn't he?

PHILLIP. Yes.

HAROLD. Have to give him credit, though. (*completely untied*) How do I look?

PHILLIP. Okay.

HAROLD. None the worse, huh.

PHILLIP. No.

HAROLD. What's that in your pocket?

PHILLIP. A shoe.

HAROLD. A woman's shoe.

PHILLIP. I found it.

HAROLD. Looks familiar. I know a woman who wore

shoes like that. She was an acrobat, female contortionist, actually . . . the positions that woman would find herself in! Boggles the imagination. You find that shoe in Chicago?

PHILLIP. No, I found it under the sofa.

HAROLD. This was a Chicago woman, she was about so high, had light blonde hair, aquiline nose, blue eyes . . . sound familiar?

PHILLIP. Yes.

HAROLD. Who's it sound like?

PHILLIP. My mother.

HAROLD. She have light blonde hair?

PHILLIP. Yes.

HAROLD. Blue eyes?

PHILLIP. Uh huh.

HAROLD. How about that!

PHILLIP. But she never was in Chicago.

HAROLD. It doesn't make any difference.

PHILLIP. She was born and died in Philadelphia.

HAROLD. If you know the type Phillip, you know the individual. Listen, you have a razor?

PHILLIP. I use Treat's.

HAROLD. Where is it?

PHILLIP. Upstairs, in the bathroom.

HAROLD. You mind if I use it?

PHILLIP. I don't mind, Harold. Treat might, though.

HAROLD. I want to be presentable when Treat comes home, Phillip. Otherwise, what would he think? (*goes upstairs, singing:*)

"If I had the wings of an angel,

Over these prison walls I would fly . . ."

(*PHILLIP runs to the stairs and looks up after him.*)

PHILLIP. (*calling*) Ahhh ya mutter!

HAROLD. (*off*) Ahhh ya mutter! Little Dead End Kid!

(*PHILLIP, smiling, looks out the window. He sees someone coming. He runs around the room in a panic. He turns towards the door. It opens. TREAT enters.*)

PHILLIP. I seen you coming. (*TREAT looks around, sees the empty chair and the rope. He grabs PHILLIP suddenly around the neck, holding him in a neck hold.*)

TREAT. Where is he?

PHILLIP. Upstairs.

TREAT. You untie him?

PHILLIP. I didn't touch him!

TREAT. Who untied him?

PHILLIP. Nobody untied him! (*TREAT pushes PHILLIP away.*)

TREAT. That guy come over here again, that actor fellow, that Errol Flynn person steal in here again and untie him?

PHILLIP. Errol Flynn didn't do it!

TREAT. I'm asking who did it! I want a straight answer!

PHILLIP. He did it himself, Treat. I swear to God!

TREAT. How did he do it?

PHILLIP. I don't know, Treat, he must be some kind of magician 'cause all of a sudden he was across the room. (*PHILLIP picks up the rope, sits on the chair and demonstrates.*) It happened right before my very eyes. His gag disappeared, his mouth began moving, and his arm come out. And pretty soon he was completely untied. (*throws rope behind him on top of TREAT*)

TREAT. What did he talk about?

PHILLIP. Nothing special. He talked about Chicago, I think, and Houdini.

TREAT. Houdini?

PHILLIP. Uh huh. He said this Houdini was a jewish fellow.

TREAT. He said that!

PHILLIP. Uh huh.

TREAT. This guy's a bullshitter!

PHILLIP. Houdini isn't jewish?

TREAT. I'm talking about this guy! (*Sound of water is heard.*) What's he doing up there?

PHILLIP. He's shaving. He wanted to be presentable when you came home.

TREAT. He's using my razor!

PHILLIP. Yes.

TREAT. The guy's taking over!

PHILLIP. He's not taking over.

TREAT. What's he doing, Phillip! I kidnapped the son of a bitch, he's supposed to be a kidnap victim, meantime he's upstairs in my bathroom, using my razor! What kind of kidnap victim is that!

PHILLIP. He's not a bad guy.

TREAT. He did some talking, huh!

PHILLIP. Yes. He told me I should wear loafers, that way I won't have to walk around with my laces untied. That way if I walk outside nobody will laugh at me 'cause nobody will ever know I can't tie a knot.

TREAT. He told you that!

PHILLIP. Yes.

TREAT. He said you should wear loafers!

PHILLIP. He said he would buy me a pair!

TREAT. Where the hell does he get his nerve! (*TREAT takes out his switchblade.*)

PHILLIP. Don't hurt him, Treat. (*TREAT opens the blade.*)

TREAT. I'll cut his heart out!

PHILLIP. He doesn't mean any harm.

TREAT. How come he didn't run away or call the police?

PHILLIP. He wanted to see you, Treat. He took a liking to you.

TREAT. He should have run away when he had the chance!

PHILLIP. He likes it here.

TREAT. What were you doing all the time his hands were appearing, all the time his hands and mouth were appearing?

PHILLIP. I didn't touch him, Treat, I was watching him, just like you said.

TREAT. Jesus!

PHILLIP. Did I do right?

TREAT. Never mind! (*puts the knife away*) He say anything about his business or any of his friends?

PHILLIP. He didn't say a word, Treat.

TREAT. He's got strange friends, this guy, peculiar type characters.

PHILLIP. What do you mean? (*HAROLD is heard singing from upstairs.*)

HAROLD. (*off*)
"If I had the wings of an angel,

Over these prison walls I would fly . . ."

(*He comes downstairs.*) Treat! I didn't hear you come in. How are you, son?

TREAT. I'm not your son!

HAROLD. You're a Dead End Kid, though, aren't you?

TREAT. No.

HAROLD. I don't mean a real Dead End Kid, for christ sake, I don't mean a literal Dead End Kid, never take me literally, Treat, you're going to have to learn not to take me literally or you're going to end right up the garden path. How the hell could you be a Dead End Kid, you would have to be 60, 70 years of age, for christ sake. (*crosses to pantry, pours himself a drink*) I mean, those Dead End Kids are old now, they've aged! Some of them are dead, others are suffering from debilitating illnesses, unrecognizable! We're talking about life and death, Treat, mortality! The human condition! You remind me of a Dead End Kid, that's why I came home with you and that's why I'm going to give you everything I have . . . I mean that, son, you name it, it's yours.

PHILLIP. Did'ja hear that, Treat!

TREAT. Shut up!

HAROLD. It was a lucky thing me meeting up with you in that downtown Philly bar. This is the first good thing that's ever happened to me in Philadelphia.

TREAT. What kind of friends you have!

HAROLD. What do you mean?

TREAT. I made some calls.

HAROLD. You have my wallet.

TREAT. That's right. I called up some people.

HAROLD. What did you say?

TREAT. I told them I had you.

HAROLD. What did they say?

TREAT. They wouldn't believe me. They thought it was some kind of a joke. They thought you put me up to it.

HAROLD. I'm not surprised.

TREAT. I told them I was serious. I said I want ransom. I told them to get it together, a million bucks!

HAROLD. What did they do?

TREAT. They laughed in my face. I said who the fuck you laughing at! I told them I'd send a piece of you back to them to prove it. I said, "How would you like to receive a finger or two in the mail as proof positive? How would you like to receive his ring finger with the ring still on it!" They said they would love to receive it. They said if it's a nice ring they would melt it down and get a few bucks for it in the open market.

HAROLD. That sounds like them.

TREAT. Another guy cursed me, he cursed you. They hung up on me.

HAROLD. I could have told you that if you asked.

TREAT. Told me what?

HAROLD. Not to call those fellows up.

TREAT. Who should I call up!

HAROLD. For ransom?

TREAT. Yea!

HAROLD. Well, you might try those orphans, they're the only family I ever had. Problem is most of them are dead now: TB, polio, hunger, poverty, violence. On second thought I wouldn't bother with those orphans.

TREAT. What about your business acquaintances?

HAROLD. What business acquaintances?

TREAT. The people whose names you got in your wallet. The people who you do business with!

HAROLD. I wouldn't exactly call them acquaintances, Treat. I hope you didn't give them your name and address.

TREAT. I didn't give them no fucking name and address.

HAROLD. That's good.

TREAT. Wadaya think I am, stupid?

HAROLD. Absolutely not.

TREAT. I'm calling up people asking for ransom, I'm gonna give my fuckin' name and address!

HAROLD. You're interested in money, huh?

TREAT. Wadaya think?

HAROLD. I think so.

TREAT. I figured we could hold you here for a nice

size ransom.

HAROLD. The best laid plans of mice and men.

TREAT. Don't give me any of that shit!

HAROLD. William Shakespeare.

TREAT. Don't give me any of that Shakespeare shit!

HAROLD. How would you like to work for me?

TREAT. For you?

HAROLD. Yes, good pay, pleasant working conditions.

TREAT. You must be kidding!

HAROLD. No, I'm serious.

TREAT. This guy's unbelievable!

HAROLD. You can be my personal bodyguard. You have a streak of violence in you, Treat. I like that.

TREAT. I'm not interested.

HAROLD. I'm offering you five hundred a week, all expenses paid.

TREAT. Shove it!

HAROLD. I'm offering you seven hundred and fifty a week. You like women?

TREAT. Sure I like women.

HAROLD. I'm offering you seven hundred and fifty dollars, plus all the women you can handle.

TREAT. Where you gonna get 'em!

HAROLD. I got a little black book. (*takes out a black book from his sock*) See this little book, worth a fortune! You talking about money, I'm showing you money right here.

TREAT. I'm self-employed.

HAROLD. You talking about your work?

TREAT. That's right!

HAROLD. You talking about those lousy nickel and dime stick-ups!

TREAT. I don't work for no one! I ain't got the temperament.

HAROLD. How come?

TREAT. It never works out.

PHILLIP. I told him you were a delinquent.

TREAT. You shut the fuck up!

HAROLD. We're going to get along real well, Treat. I'm willing to take all this into consideration. You can still be your own man.

TREAT. Forget it!

HAROLD. I'm offering you a thousand a week. (*TREAT stares at him.*) That comes to fifty-two thousand a year. That's not peanuts. And I'm talking about a position where there's room for advancement.

TREAT. How I know you're not bullshitting me!

HAROLD. Cross my heart and hope to die.

TREAT. I think you're full of shit.

HAROLD. Here's your first month's salary in advance. Four thousand dollars. Count it!

TREAT. Bring that here, Phillip. (*PHILLIP brings it over.*) Where d'ja get that?

HAROLD. My arm pit.

TREAT. I got your wallet.

HAROLD. I don't carry all my money in my wallet, Treat, just in case I get robbed. I carry money in my arm pit, my money belt, my hat, anywhere but in my wallet.

TREAT. How much you got on you?

HAROLD. Quite a bit, Treat, and access to much more. (*TREAT locks the front door.*) What do you say? Is it a deal?

TREAT. No deal.

HAROLD. One thousand dollars, that's my final offer.

TREAT. I don't take orders.

HAROLD. I'm easy to get along with.

TREAT. I kidnapped you! Who's in control here!

HAROLD. That depends.

TREAT. I'm in control. This is my house, you're my kidnap victim!

HAROLD. I understand that.

TREAT. Don't you go offering me anything, empty out your pockets, Mister!

HAROLD. That's a mistake.

TREAT. That's no mistake! Mistake was offering me a job, the mistake was showing me your money!

HAROLD. I'm offering you security for life. I'm offering you a job with a pension plan. I'm not just talking about the money I have on me. What the hell good is that! Don't you want to advance in the world!

TREAT. I'm happy where I am. Empty out your pockets.

HAROLD. I can't do that.

TREAT. You can't do that!

HAROLD. It's against my principles! (*TREAT takes out his knife and opens it.*)

TREAT. I'll cut out your fucking heart, Mister!

PHILLIP. Do what he says, Harold!

TREAT. Whoa! What are you, on a first name basis?

HAROLD. Phillip and I have an understanding. He calls me Harold. I call him Phillip.

TREAT. I don't work for nobody, you understand me! They tried to get me to work in a department store once, only trouble is I burned it down.

HAROLD. You're violent.

TREAT. Fuckin' A, Mister!

HAROLD. I like it.

TREAT. You don't hand over that money, I'm gonna cut out your heart, I swear to god!

PHILLIP. He's not kidding!

HAROLD. I'll give you money, Treat. I told you that. I'll give you way more than what I have on me, you work for me.

TREAT. I just want what you got on you. Ain't interested in anything else. You ain't gonna do anyone any good, Mister. No one wants you! I called them fucking numbers in your wallet, no one's interested in you! I don't want you either, Mister. I'm a lone operator, Phillip can tell you, strictly on my own. I don't work for no one! I don't take no orders!

HAROLD. I'll make you a bet you're going to work for me.

TREAT. This guy's crazy.

PHILLIP. He's well intentioned, Treat.

TREAT. He don't hear what I'm saying.

HAROLD. I'm going to take on the two of you, as a matter of fact. I don't intend to leave Phillip out of the picture. I'm going to work out a package deal.

TREAT. Give me your money, Mister!

HAROLD. (*continuing*) I'm talking about new clothes, fine food, fancy women! You like cashmere?

PHILLIP. I like cashmere.

HAROLD. I'm talking about only the best!

PHILLIP. Maybe we should do it, Treat.

TREAT. You're not doing nothing! You ain't goin' nowhere! This guy is dangerous, he's putting ideas in your head, making you think you can go out there like the rest of us. I don't want you dropping dead!

PHILLIP. I'm not gonna drop dead!

TREAT. I got the responsibility to take care of you. I don't want your tongue and throat swelling up and you gasping for breath!

PHILLIP. I won't gasp for breath.

HAROLD. Good boy!

TREAT. I kidnapped this fucking guy!

HAROLD. Seventeen hundred and fifty a week for the two of you, for the first six months, and a nice healthy bonus later on. I'm talking about redheaded women, Treat, redheaded, freckled women, Phillip. You like breasts?

PHILLIP. I like breasts!

HAROLD. I got just the girl for you.

PHILLIP. Let's do it, Treat!

TREAT. I'm gonna cut this fucker's heart out! (*TREAT advances on him, knife out. HAROLD pulls out a small gun, a baretta. TREAT stops.*)

HAROLD. Drop that knife, Treat, little Dead End Kid, my own little Dead End Kid, or you're going to be a dead Dead End Kid! (*TREAT drops the knife.*) First thing you do, you kidnap a man, first thing you do is frisk him. You're an amateur, a rank amateur! I'm not going to hurt you, you understand! I'm just going to hire you. You're violent, I realized that at the bar downtown, that's why I came with you. I admire violent men, men who'll stop at nothing, no limit men! You're going to work for me, Mister Treat, you're going to be my personal body guard and all around man! I'm going to train you! In a few weeks I'm going to be able to put my life in your hands . . . can you believe that! I mean right now you're filled with rage, you can hardly contain yourself. You don't even care if you live or die! You just want to get at me, am I right! Bullets don't mean a thing to you as long as you can get at me. Your life doesn't mean a thing to you, you're a wild animal! I'm going to tame you, Treat, I'm going to make you my very own! (*TREAT leaps out-of-control at HAROLD. HAROLD side-steps and hits him over the head with the handle of the gun. TREAT drops unconscious to the floor. PHILLIP has run into the closet. He peeks out.*) That's lesson number one, Phillip. It doesn't pay to lose control! You ever lose control?

PHILLIP. No! (*goes back*)

HAROLD. Come here, son! You're a good boy! Let me encourage you! You want a little encouragement, don't you! (*PHILLIP comes slowly over and stands next to*

HAROLD, who puts his arm around his shoulder, strok-ing him. They stand there, TREAT at their feet, uncon-scious.)

ACT TWO

Scene 1

Two weeks later. The house has changed. It has been cleaned up. There is more color, new drapes, rugs, plants, pictures, a liquor cart with bottles and glasses on it. On the new couch is a box with an extra long, red ribbon tied into a bow on it. One end of the ribbon trails off the couch.

PHILLIP enters from upstairs. He wears a new pair of trousers, a shirt, and a handsome sleeveless sweater. He crosses to the closet, opens the door and looks at himself in the inside door mirror. PHILLIP crosses the room and notices the box with the large bow. He stares at it. He takes hold of the long end of the ribbon and pulls it. The bow slowly unravels. PHILLIP stares at it in wonder. He climbs up on the back of the couch and lifts the lid of the box. He picks up the box and lifts out a beautiful brand new yellow loafer. He holds it up in the air. PHILLIP crosses to the window-seat with the loafer and box. He sits down and takes off his old dirty tennis shoes. He tries to put on the loafers, only he can't squeeze his feet in. PHILLIP looks up and notices some movement out the window. He rushes upstairs with his loafers.

The front door opens. TREAT enters, dressed in a stylish French suit. He is almost unrecognizable, moving smoothly and confidently. He carries a newspaper and a small paper bag which he puts down. He goes to the closet and admires himself in the inside mirror.

HAROLD. (*singing, off*)
"If I had the wings of an angel . . ."

(*HAROLD enters from the kitchen.*)

HAROLD. Treat, I didn't hear you come in. How's everything?

TREAT. Everything's fine.

HAROLD. Did you have a good day?

TREAT. I had a fabulous day! What are you drinking, Harold? (*TREAT is at the side table with the liquor.*)

HAROLD. I'm having bourbon and water.

TREAT. (*mixing*) Bourbon and water coming up!

HAROLD. Only constant thing in my life, Treat. Everything else is in flux, the whole goddamn universe is in flux except for this one constant . . . whenever liquor makes an appearance you can bet your bottom dollar, old Harold is sure to order bourbon and water.

TREAT. (*stirring drink*) That's good to know.

HAROLD. These are the facts of life, Treat, memorize them.

TREAT. They're memorized! (*TREAT offers HAROLD his drink and takes his own. HAROLD sits on the couch.*) Wadaya think of this fit, Harold?

HAROLD. It's a perfect fit.

TREAT. It ain't too tight in the crotch?

HAROLD. The crotch is fine.

TREAT. You like this suit as much as you like the beige one?

HAROLD. I like it even more.

TREAT. No kidding! Even more than the beige! (*admiring himself in mirror*) I'll tell you something, Harold, I can really get into this shit! You don't mind if I hold on to your American Express Card a few more days?

HAROLD. Be my guest. (*TREAT holds up the American Express card.*)

TREAT. This little bastard is changing my life! The

reason I wanna hold on to it, Harold, is I seen this real sharp navy blue suit in the window at Bonwit's. I realize I got the beige suit and this here baby, plus a few sport jackets and slacks, but there are seven days in the week, Harold, seven fucking days!

HAROLD. And on the seventh day we rest, Treat.

TREAT. I don't mind resting, Harold, as long as I'm resting in one of these here Pierre Cardin suits.

HAROLD. You're developing a sense of style, Treat, that's fine . . . but remember, please, everything in moderation.

TREAT. I don't know much about moderation, Harold.

HAROLD. I can see that, Treat. Did you pick up my paper?

TREAT. I sure did, Harold. I stopped off at the out-of-town newsstand.

HAROLD. Let's have it. (*TREAT hands the paper to HAROLD. He opens it.*) I appreciate that, Treat. I have a terrible nostalgia for Chicago. (*HAROLD takes out a Tiparillo. TREAT lights it. TREAT sits on the other end of the couch and takes out his own Tiparillo. They both sit in the same position, smoking.*)

TREAT. You know, Harold, it's a real pleasure picking up your Chicago Tribune and mixing you them bourbon and waters, but when are you gonna send me out on a real assignment?

HAROLD. Whenever you're ready, Treat.

TREAT. I'm ready, Harold. I've taken good care of you, haven't I?

HAROLD. I have no complaints.

TREAT. Nobody's laid a hand on you, have they?

HAROLD. Nobody.

TREAT. Not even a finger.

HAROLD. Not a finger.

TREAT. Not even a fucking mosquito bite. Am I right?

HAROLD. You're right.

TREAT. What about cold symptoms?

HAROLD. None.

TREAT. Not even a sniffle.

HAROLD. Not a sniffle. Is that because of you, Treat?

TREAT. Fucking' A, Harold! No goddamn bacteria gettin' their foot in the door while I'm around! Why, if one of those fellows from Chicago was to point a gun at you, Harold, I'd place myself between your body and that bullet.

HAROLD. You'd have to move awfully fast to do that, Treat.

TREAT. I can move fast, Harold.

HAROLD. You'd do that for me?

TREAT. Absolutely.

HAROLD. You'd sacrifice yourself?

TREAT. Whatever it takes.

HAROLD. This is amazing, Treat.

TREAT. So how 'bout it, Harold. What about a little more responsibility! Send me out on an assignment. I'm sitting here on pins and needles. (*indicates pins and needles*) Ohhh! Ahhh! (*laughs*) I got my whole new wardrobe selected.

HAROLD. There's more to it than that, Treat.

TREAT. What else is there?

HAROLD. There's your feelings.

TREAT. What's the matter with my feelings?

HAROLD. They're still uncontrollable.

TREAT. (*angry; hits couch*) Who says so!

HAROLD. What happened at Broad and Olney the other night?

TREAT. That was a week ago, Harold. I've changed since then.

HAROLD. What happened?

TREAT. I was crossing the street.

HAROLD. Go on!

TREAT. I was standing alongside of you, Harold, minding my own business, standing waiting for the red light to turn green.

HAROLD. I remember.

TREAT. When this big, fat son of a bitch walks up to me and scuffs my shoe.

HAROLD. It was an accident, Treat.

TREAT. It was my brand new alligator shoes, Harold.

HAROLD. There's no justice.

TREAT. What's that supposed to mean?

HAROLD. If you're looking for justice, you're living in the wrong century. This is the 20th century.

TREAT. I don't know if I agree with you there, Harold. Do you mind if we have a slight difference of opinion?

HAROLD. I don't mind.

TREAT. Good, 'cause when we crossed the street, I just happened to stretch out my right leg covered over by my brand new Pierre Cardin trousers and that s.o.b. happened to trip over it and land on his big fat fucking face. (*pause*) So you see, Harold, sometimes, every so often, there is justice.

HAROLD. You believe in an eye for an eye, in other words.

TREAT. I don't know, Harold, I got these feelings! Some s.o.b. comes along and scuffs my shoe, these feelings rise up in me. What am I supposed to do with them!

HAROLD. Did you ever try counting to ten?

TREAT. Counting to ten? (*PHILLIP enters carrying the loafers.*)

HAROLD. You know, one, two, three, four, et cetera . . .

TREAT. You must be kidding.

HAROLD. I'm serious. It's a first step. It gives your emotions time to settle down.

TREAT. I can see if you tell me to count to a thousand or maybe even ten thousand, that way the cock sucker is outta sight. If I count to a million, he's outta the fucking country!

HAROLD. You know who you remind me of, Treat? Fred. He didn't believe in moderation either.

TREAT. Who's Fred?

HAROLD. He was an orphan, just like me. We were newsboys together, south side of Chicago. Little motherless newsboys standing in the cold, yelling "EXTRA! EXTRA! READ ALL ABOUT IT!", fighting our way from the outskirts of the city to the very heart of Chicago . . . Little motherless fucking orphans fighting tooth and nail, block after block, fighting for each and every corner. That's the free enterprise system, Treat. That's Capitalism! (*PHILLIP sits on the floor, listening to the story.*) We use to watch the Dead End Kids together every Sunday matinee. He died of pneumonia though, one frigid January day. Freezing wind coming off the Lake. I had a Chicago Tribune tucked away inside my front shirt and one in my back. That's an old newsboys' trick, protects you from the elements. Only thing is on this particular day Fred sold the Tribune covering his chest. I told him he was crazy, temperature was dropping rapidly. He turned around and sold the other Tribune covering his back. Moderation, Treat, moderation! Poor motherless newsboy, totally exposed on that frigid January day. Had a hacking cough by the time we got back to the Orphanage. Later on a raging fever — the next morning he was gone.

PHILLIP. Gone?

HAROLD. We buried him in the Orphans' Cemetery. I'm giving you a lesson in moderation, boys, and also economics, the profit motive. How far a man will go for financial gain. (*HAROLD crosses behind TREAT and puts his hand on his shoulder. TREAT pulls away. HAROLD stares at him a moment, picks up his drink and crosses to the window seat. He looks out the window.*) I wished to god I could get out of this lousy business. I wish to god I could go back to Chicago.

PHILLIP. Why can't you, Harold?

HAROLD. There's a widow there, lovely little widow lady. Have I mentioned her?

PHILLIP. No.

HAROLD. I haven't seen her in years. Been traveling . . . Detroit, Pittsburgh, Baltimore . . .

PHILLIP. Why can't you go back to Chicago, Harold?

HAROLD. I burned some bridges, Phillip. It's a real tragedy. There are a number of men who are looking for me. (*PHILLIP tries to put the loafer on.*)

PHILLIP. I never been to Chicago.

HAROLD. You're missing something.

PHILLIP. I've never been outta North Philadelphia.

HAROLD. What are you doing with that loafer, Phillip?

PHILLIP. I can't get it on my foot, Harold. It won't fit.

HAROLD. Why don't you try this? (*HAROLD takes a shoe horn from the shoe box and holds it up. A long pause.*)

PHILLIP. (*in wonder*) What is it?

HAROLD. A shoe horn. Press down, Phillip. (*PHILLIP places his foot in the loafer and it slips on.*)

PHILLIP. It worked!

HAROLD. Of course it worked! (*hands PHILLIP shoe*

horn) You do the other. (*PHILLIP puts the other loafer on, himself. He walks around the room.*) How do they feel?

PHILLIP. They feel wonderful, Harold. They feel like I'm walking on air. (*PHILLIP runs off, upstairs.*)

HAROLD. (*calling after*) You're doing real well, Phillip. I'm proud of you.

TREAT. What about me, Harold. How am I doing?

HAROLD. I'm not sure, Treat. (*studies TREAT a moment, then stretches out his arm*) Why don't you come over here, son. Let me give you some encouragement. (*A long pause. TREAT doesn't move.*)

TREAT. I don't need no encouragement, Harold. I just need an assignment.

HAROLD. I'll think about it, Treat. (*HAROLD crosses to the kitchen, off. PHILLIP comes downstairs, moving joyfully on the loafers.*)

TREAT. You and Harold are getting as thick as thieves, ain't you?

PHILLIP. Harold's no thief.

TREAT. Oh, no? Then how come he just got done telling us he can't go back to Chicago? How come he just finished saying he was on the lam.

PHILLIP. He didn't say he was on a lamb.

TREAT. Not on *a* lamb, on *the* lam.

PHILLIP. He never said he was on any kind of a lamb.

TREAT. Didn't you ever hear that expression before?

PHILLIP. I heard that expression. I heard 'em say it in the late night movie, "The Black Hand," starring Cornel Wilde.

TREAT. Well, what did you think? You think Cornel Wilde was on a lamb?

PHILLIP. Yes.

TREAT. What was he doing on a lamb?

PHILLIP. (*pause, thinks*) Maybe he was sitting on it.

TREAT. Sitting on a lamb, huh?

PHILLIP. Something like that.

TREAT. You got an imagination, Phillip. I gotta hand it to you. (*picks up the paper bag he brought home*) I got something for you.

PHILLIP. Wadaya got?

TREAT. Something real nice. Come over here, Phillip.

PHILLIP. No.

TREAT. What's the matter?

PHILLIP. Nothing's the matter.

TREAT. Well, come on over then. I wanna show you. (*PHILLIP hesitates, shakes his head.*)

TREAT. You think I'm gonna do something, is that it?

PHILLIP. Yes.

TREAT. You think your big brother Treat is gonna pull a fast one?

PHILLIP. Yes.

TREAT. I've always taken good care of you, haven't I? And today's no exception. (*pulls out a large bottle from the bag*) Look! An extra large bottle of Hellman's Real Mayonnaise! I knew you had a taste in your mouth for it.

PHILLIP. I don't have a taste in my mouth for it anymore, though, Treat.

TREAT. Wadaya mean?

PHILLIP. I'm actually sick and tired of Hellman's.

TREAT. Wadaya saying?

PHILLIP. I have a taste in my mouth for other things, Treat.

TREAT. What other things!

PHILLIP. I have a taste in my mouth for corn beef and cabbage, the way Harold prepares it, nice and thick and juicy, and dipped in dark brown mustard. You want me to cut you off a slice? (*TREAT shakes his head 'no.'*)

You sure, Treat? I'm gonna cut myself off a slice right this very minute. (*TREAT doesn't answer.*) If you change your mind, Treat, you just let me know. (*PHILLIP crosses to kitchen. Sound of PHILLIP and HAROLD talking, off. TREAT stands a long moment, fingering the bottle of mayonnaise.*)

SCENE 2

A couple of days later. Evening. PHILLIP at the table, a napkin tucked in his shirt, eats a bowl of soup. A large soup tureen with a ladle is nearby. HAROLD is at the window looking down the street. PHILLIP, sitting perfectly straight in the chair, takes a spoonful of soup and brings it slowly to his mouth. He doesn't bend over. The soup spills on his napkin. He tries again. It spills again. HAROLD turns.

HAROLD. How is it?

PHILLIP. Mmmmm. (*He hasn't had any. HAROLD crosses over to him and bends PHILLIP's head over. He tastes it.*)

HAROLD. Delicious, huh?

PHILLIP. Mmmmm.

HAROLD. It's bouilabaisse.

PHILLIP. (*eating*) Bouilabaisse?

HAROLD. Congratulations, Phillip. That's French. You just spoke the French language. Tomorrow we're having gazpacho. You're going to be multi-lingual by the end of the week. Do you believe that?

PHILLIP. Yes.

HAROLD. Good. You have a simple faith, Phillip. I admire a man with a simple faith. Do you have any idea what's in this soup?

PHILLIP. I seen you throw in that lobster, Harold, plus all them clams and scallops and them tiny little bay shrimp.

HAROLD. Do you realize how long it's taken for each of these individual species to evolve?

PHILLIP. I got no idea.

HAROLD. Guess.

PHILLIP. A thousand years?

HAROLD. Wrong! Millions! Hundreds of millions of years. In the beginning, Phillip, we were all the same, we were undifferentiated creatures. And then gradually different life forms evolved and separated themselves from the rest. They became individualized, Phillip. They became entirely different species. And do you know now what's happening in your stomach?

PHILLIP. What's happening?

HAROLD. A miracle is taking place.

PHILLIP. In my stomach?

HAROLD. Yes, right now in your stomach, a genuine miracle. If you were catholic we could have the Pope consecrate this spot. It would become a shrine. Millions of Pilgrims would come and pay their respects because in your stomach all those highly individualized species are rapidly disappearing. Evolution is reversing itself. They're losing their identity, Phillip. They're becoming something else.

PHILLIP. What are they becoming?

HAROLD. You, Phillip, part of you.

PHILLIP. Me?

HAROLD. Yes. Your digestive juices are right this moment attacking all of them little shrimp and clams and scallops, all those highly individualized life forms that it took millions of years to evolve. (*PHILLIP pushes the soup bowl away. He crosses to the couch.*)

PHILLIP. (*lying down*) I ain't attacking anybody.

HAROLD. Unconscious processes, Phillip. What's the matter?

PHILLIP. I ain't hungry.

HAROLD. You left your whole lobster.

PHILLIP. I got no appetite.

HAROLD. You're perspiring, Phillip. Maybe I better open a window. Let in some air.

PHILLIP. Don't do that, Harold!

HAROLD. Why not?

PHILLIP. I ain't allowed to breathe in the night air.

HAROLD. Who says so?

PHILLIP. Treat. He says it's even worse than the day.

HAROLD. What do you think we're standing in right now, Phillip?

PHILLIP. I don't know.

HAROLD. We're standing in the middle of the night.

PHILLIP. No.

HAROLD. You can't keep out the night. It slips in through the door. It comes in through the cracks. All of North Philadelphia is covered by the night, Phillip. The whole Western Hemisphere, as a matter of fact. (*He opens the window. PHILLIP hides, covers his face.*) Come over here, Phillip. Let me give you some encouragement. (*PHILLIP goes over to HAROLD, who holds him a moment. PHILLIP puts his head out the window.*) How do you feel now?

PHILLIP. I don't know.

HAROLD. Let me see your face.

PHILLIP. Is it swollen?

HAROLD. No, it's perfectly normal. How is your breathing?

PHILLIP. My breathing's okay.

HAROLD. Breathing's fine. You're not gasping for air?

PHILLIP. No. (*HAROLD hits PHILLIP on the back.*)

HAROLD. Windpipe's open!

PHILLIP. Yes.

HAROLD. No asthma, am I right?

PHILLIP. You're right.

HAROLD. Congratulations, Phillip. You're making real progress. (*PHILLIP jumps up on the pantry shelf and sticks half his body out the window.*) I think you're ready for a walk.

PHILLIP. A walk?

HAROLD. I don't mean right this moment, maybe tomorrow.

PHILLIP. I don't think I can do that, Harold.

HAROLD. Why not?

PHILLIP. Because once I go out, once I turn the corner and lose sight of the house, why I might never find my way back again.

HAROLD. You know your address, though, don't you?

PHILLIP. I know my address all right. Sixty-forty North Camac Street. Only thing is, Treat says, you go to the wrong person and ask directions why they might even slit your throat.

HAROLD. I have something for you, Phillip. You'll never have to worry about getting lost again.

PHILLIP. What's what? (*HAROLD takes out a folded map. He opens it with a flourish.*)

HAROLD. It's a map of Philadelphia.

PHILLIP. I never seen one before. (*PHILLIP holds it.*)

HAROLD. You never saw a map?

PHILLIP. I seen a map of the United States of America, but I never knew there were maps of individual cities and streets.

HAROLD. There are maps of everything, Phillip. There's a map of the whole planet Earth, which is third from the sun. There's a map of the Milky Way galaxy which we are a part of.

PHILLIP. We are?

HAROLD. Yes. We're tucked away safe and sound at the very edge of the Milky Way which is swimming in the great ocean of space. We're circling the sun, Phillip. We're in the Western Hemisphere, North American Continent, State of Pennsylvania, City of Philadelphia. See this! (*HAROLD points to the map.*)

PHILLIP. Yes.

HAROLD. Know what it is?

PHILLIP. What is it?

HAROLD. North Philadelphia!

PHILLIP. Really!

HAROLD. Right over here. And this is Camac Street.

PHILLIP. This is Camac Street.

HAROLD. The sixty-forty block. I'm going to circle it, Phillip. You'll never get lost again. You're going to know exactly where you are in time and space.

PHILLIP. Harold, can I keep it?

HAROLD. It's yours, Phillip. (*PHILLIP crumbles it under his shirt.*)

PHILLIP. I know where I am now, Harold! I know exactly where I am! (*PHILLIP embraces HAROLD.*)

HAROLD. Good boy!

(*The front door opens. TREAT enters in suit and tie, carrying a briefcase. He sees them and slams the door shut.*)

TREAT. I'm starving. What's for dinner!

PHILLIP. (*crosses to him*) Bouilabaisse.

TREAT. What you say to me!

PHILLIP. It's French, Treat. I can speak the French language now.

HAROLD. Treat! I was beginning to have second

thoughts about sending you on an assignment. You're late.

TREAT. Nothing to worry about, Harold. (*TREAT takes out stocks and bonds from the briefcase. PHILLIP quietly closes the window.*) Ten thousand shares of A.T.&T., 25 thousand shares of Mobil Oil. Stocks, bonds, just like you wanted. (*dumps them on table*)

HAROLD. This is wonderful, Treat. (*looking through stocks*) But why did it take you so long? It's after seven.

TREAT. You know the traffic, Harold. (*removes his jacket, revealing shoulder holster and gun*)

HAROLD. Did you take the West River Drive?

TREAT. I went up Broad Street. (*PHILLIP crosses into the kitchen.*)

HAROLD. Broad Street. How come?

TREAT. I took the Broad Street bus, Harold. (*TREAT mixes himself a drink.*)

HAROLD. Why did you do that? You were supposed to take a cab there and back.

TREAT. It's a long story.

HAROLD. I gave you specific instructions, Treat. I didn't want anyone following you home. (*HAROLD crosses to the window and looks out.*)

TREAT. No one followed me, Harold, honest to God. I just felt real conspicuous being chauffeured around. That's why I asked the cab driver to pull over and let me off.

HAROLD. That cab driver was working on a commission, Treat. This is the free enterprise system, individual initiative, et cetera. You took money out of that poor cabbie's mouth, but you didn't put it in the mouth of the bus driver.

TREAT. Whose mouth did I put it into?

HAROLD. That bus driver works for the Philadelphia Transportation Company. He has a fixed income. He doesn't give a flying fuck whether the bus was filled or empty.

TREAT. It was filled, Harold.

HAROLD. I'm giving you a lesson in economic realities, Treat.

TREAT. I appreciate that, Harold, and next time I'm definitely gonna take a Yellow Cab 'cause that Broad Street bus was a real bitch.

HAROLD. Oh, why is that, Treat? (*PHILLIP enters and sits at the table.*)

TREAT. There was this big black guy sitting there, must have been a basketball player. He was sitting in his seat, Harold, but he had his long legs spread out wide. (*demonstrates on couch*)

HAROLD. Go on.

TREAT. He's squeezing the life out of the passengers on either side of him. There was a guy in a business suit to his right. I didn't give a fuck about him, but to his left was this sweet little old lady who was all scrunched up.

HAROLD. What happened?

TREAT. All along the bus, people scrunched up, people turning all shades of blue 'cause this black fellow wouldn't move.

HAROLD. What did you do?

TREAT. You wanna hear the story?

HAROLD. I'm very interested in the story.

TREAT. The little old lady finally gets up and leaves the bus.

HAROLD. Yes.

TREAT. So I sit down.

HAROLD. That's a mistake.

TREAT. It's a long ride up Broad Street, Harold.

HAROLD. Go on!

TREAT. So I'm sitting in my seat, right, and there's no room, so I figure maybe if I apply a little leg pressure he'll ease up.

HAROLD. And did he?

TREAT. The guy doesn't budge, Harold. So I apply more pressure. I mean I'm straining. My leg is straining against this guy's huge black leg.

HAROLD. And then what?

TREAT. He lets on nothing's happening. The guy is like the fucking Rock of Gibralter.

HAROLD. You're in a situation, Treat. I warned you about this!

TREAT. I had no choice.

HAROLD. You didn't have to sit down.

TREAT. I thought he would shift over.

HAROLD. The man isn't going to shift over. You knew that, Treat. Let's lay our cards on the table. In your heart of hearts you knew there was no way that man was going to shift over. (*a pause*)

TREAT. You're right, Harold. In my heart of hearts I knew that.

HAROLD. And you sit down anyway?

TREAT. I sat down because the son of a bitch was squeezing the life outta all the passengers. Somebody had to do something.

HAROLD. You're talking about justice again.

TREAT. That's right! (*sits on the back of the couch, takes out his gun*) I turned to the guy and I said, "Guess what's in my right hand?" The guy didn't know how to respond. He figured I was gonna say something about his leg.

HAROLD. Go on!

TREAT. It's a good story, huh, Harold?

HAROLD. Go on, Treat.

TREAT. I said, "My hand is pressed against a pistol which is aimed directly at your black heart."

HAROLD. You said that!

TREAT. I told him I was gonna count to ten, just like you taught me, Harold. I said, "You don't close your legs and give me some breathing space by the count of ten I'm gonna press my index finger against the trigger of this semi-automatic pistol and a bullet is gonna explode right through my jacket and into your big black heart."

HAROLD. This is unbelievable!

TREAT. I want you to understand something, Harold. I'm not prejudiced. I mean, I would have done the same whether it was a chink, a dago or any of them other ethnic bastards.

HAROLD. What did he do?

TREAT. He sat there quietly for a moment and then I began counting, just like you said . . . one, two, three, four . . . and by the time I got to five he was out of the bus.

HAROLD. What would you have done, Treat, if you reached ten and he still didn't move.

TREAT. That wasn't the case.

HAROLD. I'm discussing a hypothetical situation.

TREAT. I don't know nothing about them hypothetical situations.

HAROLD. You knew when you sat down it was going to be a case of wills.

TREAT. I knew that. I admitted that, yes.

HAROLD. So let's go one step further. You get to ten, he doesn't budge, what do you do?

TREAT. He doesn't budge?

HAROLD. Not an inch.

TREAT. You want the truth or do you want me to bullshit you?

HAROLD. I want the truth.

TREAT. I press the trigger, Harold. I blow the bastard's brains all over the Broad Street bus. (*He pretend shoots: "Boom! Boom!" And falls on couch in mock death.*)

HAROLD. I see.

TREAT. Serves him fucking right.

HAROLD. Then what?

TREAT. Wadaya mean, then what?

HAROLD. He's dead, blood is everywhere, blood is all over your new suit, blood is all over the people around you who are screaming. What do you do?

TREAT. (*sitting up*) I didn't think about that.

HAROLD. You're carrying a briefcase filled with hundreds of thousands of dollars worth of negotiable stocks and bonds. What do you do then!

TREAT. Jesus, Harold, I don't know. I run, I suppose. I jump out of the bus and run down Broad Street.

HAROLD. You're running along Broad Street covered from head to foot with blood.

TREAT. Jesus Christ! This is terrible!

HAROLD. I trusted you, Treat. I relied on you.

TREAT. I'm sorry, Harold. I didn't think.

HAROLD. You're not ready to go on an assignment. You don't know how to control yourself. Let me have the gun. (*a pause*)

TREAT. I can do it now, Harold, I swear to God. (*HAROLD holds out his hand. A long pause.*)

HAROLD. Let me have the gun, Treat. (*TREAT hands HAROLD the gun and holster.*)

TREAT. I can do it. I understand the principle.

HAROLD. You understand the principle?

TREAT. Yes. Give me another chance.

HAROLD. You want another chance?

TREAT. Yes.

HAROLD. Okay, I'm going to give you one more chance.

TREAT. I appreciate this, Harold.

HAROLD. You're on the bus again. Phillip, did you hear the story?

PHILLIP. Yes.

HAROLD. (*pulls chair out*) Sit over here. You play the black man.

PHILLIP. (*black accent*) I'm the black man!

HAROLD. You're the black man and you won't budge for anything, okay?

PHILLIP. I won't fucking budge, Harold. (*HAROLD places another chair next to PHILLIP.*)

HAROLD. You sit next to him, Treat.

(*TREAT walks over. PHILLIP has spread his legs out across the other chair. There is hardly any room. TREAT squeezes in next to him. PHILLIP sings ala Louie Armstrong.*)

PHILLIP.
"If I had the wings of an angel,
Over these prison walls I would fly . . ."
(*PHILLIP continues singing.*)

TREAT. He's singing, Harold.

HAROLD. That's all right.

TREAT. What the fuck is he singing about? The black guy didn't sing!

HAROLD. It's okay, Treat. Concentrate on your part.

TREAT. I'm concentrating!

HAROLD. All right. You're next to him, the bus is crowded, you have no room. What do you do?

TREAT. (*pause, thinks*) I don't do anything, Harold, 'cause I don't wanna create a situation.

HAROLD. Your balls are turning blue, Treat. What do you do?

TREAT. My balls are blue?

HAROLD. Uh huh. What do you do?

TREAT. Maybe I give him a little nudge, you know, just to test the waters.

HAROLD. Are you doing that?

TREAT. (*pushes*) I'm giving him a little nudge.

HAROLD. Okay! Go on!

TREAT. (*harder*) The bastard won't move.

HAROLD. What do you do?

TREAT. (*stops, controls himself*) I don't do nothing, Harold, 'cause I got it all under control now. I let up the pressure and I just sit there with my blue balls until we get to downtown Philadelphia.

HAROLD. Okay, the bus is jam-packed and a cripple comes on.

TREAT. A cripple?

HAROLD. Yes, a horribly deformed cripple, a soldier, a Vietnam veteran, his testacles blown off in the war.

TREAT. Oh, Jesus, his testacles!

HAROLD. The man is a walking nightmare, every step is terrible agony. I'll play that man. (*begins an extreme limp*) Oh, my god! I'm in pain. Someone please give me a seat! (*TREAT jumps up.*)

TREAT. Here, Mister, take mine!

HAROLD. I can't sit there. There's no room.

TREAT. Why don't you move over a little bit, buddy. This guy's a vet!

PHILLIP. (*black accent*) Why don't you take a flying shit!

TREAT. What did you say?

PHILLIP. I'm not going to move a fucking inch.

TREAT. The guy didn't talk like that, Harold. The guy didn't open up his mouth!

HAROLD. Help me, please, somebody. The medicine is wearing off.

TREAT. The medicine is wearing off! Oh, Jesus, Harold, I can't stand it!

HAROLD. Please, Mister, I'm begging you, a little mercy.

PHILLIP. Why don't you go tell your mother she wants you!

TREAT. Harold, I'm trying! I'm really trying! What am I supposed to do!

PHILLIP. (*singing*)
"If I had the wings of an angel,
Over these prison walls I would fly."

TREAT. The feelings are building up again, Harold. Help me! (*lets out a bloodcurdling scream and moves towards PHILLIP.*) AHHHHHHH! (*He stops and begins flailing at himself, moving around the room. He falls to the floor, unconscious.*)

PHILLIP. What happened?

HAROLD. He fainted.

PHILLIP. Treat?

HAROLD. His feelings were too much for him. He'll be alright, though. (*HAROLD kneels beside him and begins to stroke his shoulders. TREAT moans.*) Poor little Dead End Kid. You tried, though, didn't you. (*He continues to stroke him. TREAT wakes up.*)

TREAT. What are you doing?

HAROLD. I'm giving you some encouragement . . . (*TREAT pulls away.*)

TREAT. I don't want any encouragement!

HAROLD. Don't be scared, son.

TREAT. (*backing away*) I'm not your son, I don't need you! (*HAROLD moves towards him. TREAT moves away, frightened.*) Stay away! Don't come near me!

Don't touch me! (*TREAT, backing away, runs out into the night.*)

SCENE 3

An hour later. PHILLIP sits at the window seat looking out at the night. HAROLD comes down the stairs. He fixes himself a drink.

HAROLD. Any sign of Treat?

PHILLIP. No sign, Harold.

HAROLD. I hope I wasn't too hard on him.

PHILLIP. You know sometimes late at night, Harold, I come downstairs and watch the sun come up over Camac Street.

HAROLD. (*sits at table*) That's quite a trick.

PHILLIP. Pretty soon it crosses the heavens and then night comes.

HAROLD. That's one trick Houdini never learned.

PHILLIP. When night comes something amazing happens, Harold.

HAROLD. What is that?

PHILLIP. The street lamps go on all along Camac Street. I called Treat's attention to that fact. I said, "Look, Treat, ain't that a miracle, first the sun comes up and crosses North Philadelphia and disappears, and then the street lamps go on lighting up all of Camac Street."

HAROLD. What did he say?

PHILLIP. He said, "It's no fucking miracle. It's General Electric!"

HAROLD. Don't listen to him, Phillip. It is a miracle. Each of those lights have inside of themselves a little piece of the sun.

PHILLIP. That's how I see it, Harold.

HAROLD. You're a wise man, Phillip. Never doubt your own instincts.

PHILLIP. I never will, Harold.

HAROLD. Good boy. (*HAROLD stares at PHILLIP a long moment and then crosses to the kitchen. PHILLIP walks over to the TV set and turns it on. The sound track from the old thirties film, "CHARGE OF THE LIGHT BRIGADE," starring Errol Flynn, is heard.* PHILLIP squats, engrossed, listening. HAROLD enters wearing a zippered jacket and carrying another jacket. He crosses to PHILLIP.*) Slip in your arm, Phillip. (*PHILLIP slips in his arm, still engrossed in the film.*) Now the other.

(*PHILLIP slips in his other arm. HAROLD, behind him, places an old-fashioned 1930's cap on his head. PHILLIP reaches up and touches it in amazement. HAROLD crosses to the door and opens it. He stands waiting. PHILLIP turns slowly and crosses to the front door and walks out. HAROLD behind him, snaps off the light and closes the door. The sound of the bugle charge in "CHARGE OF THE LIGHT BRIGADE," from the TV. TREAT appears at the pantry window. He presses his face against the glass, looking in. He opens the window with his knife and climbs in. He has been drinking and is disheveled. He takes off his shoes on the pantry counter. He crosses unsteadily into the kitchen. He reappears a moment later, crosses to the stairs and listens. He closes his knife and puts it in his pocket. He crosses to the bar and downs a swig of liquor. TREAT's attention is drawn to the TV set. Errol*)

---

*Note: permission to produce ORPHANS does not include rights to use this material in production. Such rights ought to be procured by individual producers from the copyright owner of the material.

*Flynn is speaking. TREAT crosses slowly and bends
down, staring directly into the TV tube. Errol Flynn
continues speaking.*)

TREAT. Son of a bitch. (*He snaps the TV set off. He
crosses to the foot of the stairs and listens. He crosses to
the sofa and sits down, exhausted. He feels something
under his seat and wiggles around trying to make himself comfortable. He puts his hand under the cushion
and pulls out a book. He opens it.*) Son of a bitch! (*He
reaches in again and pulls out another book and then
another. He feels something else under there, something
unusual. He pulls out the red high-heeled shoe.*) Son of
a fucking bitch! (*He stuffs back the books and shoe. He
crosses to the stairs and walks up. A moment passes.
Calling, off:*) Phillip? (*TREAT descends the stairs
slowly, puzzled. He crosses to the middle of the room
and looks around.*) Come on out, Phillip. I ain't in the
mood for no hide-and-go-seek games. (*He looks around,
his gaze stops at the closet. He crosses over and opens
the door. He enters. A long moment. TREAT reappears,
holding almost absentmindedly, one of the mother's
coats . . . a big furry one. He walks across the room,
holding it. He stops and speaks softly, almost inaudi-
bly.*) Phillip. (*TREAT crosses to the kitchen table and
sits on one of the chairs, holding the coat. He calls out
once more, softly . . .*) Phillip.

SCENE 4

*Two hours later. TREAT sitting in the exact same place.
He is clutching the coat tightly to himself.
The front door opens. PHILLIP enters in his jacket and
cap, carrying some flowers.*

PHILLIP. What's the matter, Treat? You look pale.
(*no answer*) You look white as a ghost. You want an

aspirin? (*no answer*) I'll get you a Bayer aspirin. (*He starts into the kitchen.*)

TREAT. I don't want a Bayer aspirin.

PHILLIP. What about Excedrin?

TREAT. I don't want any fucking aspirins! (*PHILLIP notices the coat.*)

PHILLIP. Wadaya doing with that coat? (*TREAT looks down and realizes he is holding the coat.*) That's Mom's coat, Treat. How come you're holding Mom's coat. (*TREAT drops the coat on the floor.*)

TREAT. Where were you?

PHILLIP. I was out. I took a walk, Treat. I walked all the way over to Broad and Olney.

TREAT. Where's Harold?

PHILLIP. I don't know, Treat. One moment he was with me and the next moment he was gone.

TREAT. Where is the son of a bitch!

PHILLIP. He seen these fellows from Chicago, Treat. They were walking right behind us, and he said, "You keep walking, Phillip, I'll see you later," and then I seen him walk to the corner and he disappeared.

TREAT. Wadaya mean disappeared?

PHILLIP. He wasn't there.

TREAT. He didn't disappear, Phillip, he just turned the corner!

PHILLIP. Oh.

TREAT. He was just out of sight!

PHILLIP. Anyway, I ain't seen him. (*PHILLIP walks into the kitchen.*)

TREAT. I WANT HIM OUT OF HERE, PHILLIP! I WANT HIM THE FUCK OUT! (*TREAT, upset, tries to compose himself. He takes a swig from the liquor bottle. He calls off to PHILLIP.*) I seen a friend of yours.

PHILLIP. (*off*) What?

TREAT. I SAID I JUST NOW SEEN A FRIEND OF YOURS! (*PHILLIP returns with an empty large bottle of Hellman's Mayonnaise. He places the flowers inside.*)

PHILLIP. Who'd you see?

TREAT. I seen an old re-run of the "Charge of the Light Brigade," starring none other than your old buddy, Errol Flynn.

PHILLIP. He's not my buddy. I hardly know him.

TREAT. He's a handsome son of a bitch though, isn't he?

PHILLIP. He's handsome, all right.

TREAT. Did you see the film?

PHILLIP. Yes.

TREAT. I bet there's not a goddamn film you haven't seen. I mean, I bet you're a fucking walking encyclopedia of the film industry.

PHILLIP. I seen every one of his films.

TREAT. That's what I'm saying. I'm also wondering what a famous movie star like him is doing hanging around North Philly, sneaking into people's houses, underlining words, underlining sentences, even phrases.

PHILLIP. I wouldn't know.

TREAT. Here I am sitting watching Errol Flynn on horseback, leading the famous Charge of the Ten Thousand, when suddenly I hear something. Wadaya think I heard?

PHILLIP. I don't know, Treat.

TREAT. I'm watching Errol Flynn on TV and at the same time out of the corner of my eye I see the bastard sneaking around my house. The fucker is a glutton for punishment, Phillip. I mean, the last time he was here he hadda jump out a second story window. He could've broken his neck, could've ruined his career. Hollywood ain't interested in no leading man with a broken neck. What kinda parts is he gonna play . . . broken neck parts! Corpses! Maybe even the Hunchback of Notre Dame! He must have been hanging around here for years, Phillip! Look! (*pulls out the books from under the couch*) Life on the Mississippi, by Mark Twain! The Count of fucking Monte Cristo! The Arabian Nights! Books, books, everywhere and in each of these books, underlined words, thousands of underlined words. And look what else I found! (*pulls out the red shoe*) Imagine that! All this time we was thinking she was some kind of one-legged tramp when all along she had two legs. She does have an unusual problem though. This is a shoe for a right foot and the shoe we threw out that window was for another right foot, which leads me to believe that this woman has two right feet. What the fuck does she look like, Phillip, some kind of awful monster roaming the Philadelphia streets, leaning to the right. (*He hurls the shoe against the wall. He fixes himself a drink.*) I think that's the last of Errol Flynn, though, Phillip.

PHILLIP. Wadaya mean?

TREAT. I caught him dead to rights. He's not gonna bother us ever again.

PHILLIP. What did you do?

TREAT. I cut off his hands. (*pause*) I had no choice. You didn't happen to see him on the way home, did you?

PHILLIP. No.

TREAT. Let me give you a fuller description . . . a handsome looking fellow with a pencil thin mustache, a movie star, running along Camac Street with two bloody stumps.

PHILLIP. I didn't see him, Treat.

TREAT. You didn't see no trail of blood?

PHILLIP. I didn't see no trail of blood, but I seen other things.

TREAT. What other things you seen?

PHILLIP. Plenty of other things. (*faces him*) He's got rights, Treat.

TREAT. What rights you talking about?

PHILLIP. He's got certain unalienable rights. He's got the right to Life, Liberty and the Pursuit of Happiness.

TREAT. Who told you that? Harold!

PHILLIP. It's in the Declaration of Independence, Treat! (*pause*) I took a walk tonight. I walked over to Broad and Olney.

TREAT. I'm not interested.

PHILLIP. I was breathing okay, Treat. I didn't have no allergy reaction like you said I would.

TREAT. I was watching out for you.

PHILLIP. I took the subway, Treat.

TREAT. I don't want to hear no more!

PHILLIP. Harold told me the secret. You can stand all day at the turnstile putting in nickles and dimes, you can say Open Assasime and all kinds of words, but it won't do any good unless you have one of these magical coins. (*PHILLIP pulls out a coin. He hands it to him.*)

TREAT. That's a token!

PHILLIP. If Harold hadn't given me one I never would have been able to take that ride.

TREAT. It's a fucking Philadelphia subway token! (*throws it away*)

PHILLIP. I know that.

TREAT. Anyone can buy one of those lousy tokens. All you gotta do is walk up to any token booth.

PHILLIP. You never told me about them token booths! You never told me about nothing!

TREAT. I had other things on my mind. I was making us a living. I had the responsibility.

PHILLIP. You told me I would die if I went outside.

TREAT. Don't you remember what happened last time?

Your face swelled up, your tongue was hanging outta your mouth. You couldn't breathe! (*PHILLIP runs to the pantry window and throws it open. He runs across the living room to the window seat and throws open that window. He flings the door open wide.*)

PHILLIP. I can breathe, Treat. Look! My tongue ain't hanging out. My face ain't swollen! (*pause*) I walked over to Broad and Olney tonight, Treat. I seen people walking, and I heard children laughing.

TREAT. I told you I wasn't interested.

PHILLIP. I wasn't scared no more 'cause Harold gave me something. (*PHILLIP takes out the map.*) He gave me this! (*opens the map*)

TREAT. It's a map! It's a map of fucking Philadelphia!

PHILLIP. You never gave me no map, Treat. You never told me I could find my way!

TREAT. I didn't want us separated. I didn't want anything happening to you.

PHILLIP. Nothing's gonna happen to me, Treat, 'cause I know where I am now. I know where I am, and you ain't ever gonna take that away from me.

TREAT. Where are you?

PHILLIP. I'M AT SIXTY-FORTY NORTH CAMAC STREET, IN PHILADELPHIA, TREAT! I'M ON THE EASTERN EDGE OF THE STATE OF PENNSYL-VANIA IN THE UNITED STATES OF AMERICA! I'M ON THE NORTH AMERICAN CONTINENT, ON THE PLANET EARTH, IN THE MILKY WAY GALAXY, SWIMMING IN THE GREAT OCEAN OF SPACE! I'M SAFE AND SOUND AT THE VERY EDGE OF THE MILKY WAY! THAT'S WHERE I AM, TREAT! (*A long pause. PHILLIP picks up the map and tags TREAT.*) And you're it, Treat.

TREAT. No.

PHILLIP. You're fucking it. Game's over. (*PHILLIP crosses to the stairs, closes the door, and begins to walk up the stairs. TREAT calls to him.*)

TREAT. PHILLIP! PHILLIP! (*PHILLIP stops.*) How come Harold never mentioned that there are people out there who might just walk right up to you and ... (*walks up to PHILLIP, pulls map out of his hand*) steal your map.

PHILLIP. Give me that, Treat!

TREAT. Malicious people.

PHILLIP. I'm warning you, Treat!

TREAT. Terrible people. (*TREAT begins to tear the map up into little pieces. PHILLIP grabs him from behind and wrestles with him. TREAT continues to rip the map.*) People who got no scruples.

PHILLIP. Stop that! (*TREAT and PHILLIP wrestle. TREAT grabs PHILLIP's head and throws him to the floor.*)

TREAT. (*on top of him*) How come he didn't warn you! (*TREAT is strangling PHILLIP. He stops suddenly and pulls away in horror. He backs up against the wall and turns and faces it. PHILLIP, on the floor, moves to the torn pieces of the map.*)

PHILLIP. You shouldn't've done that, Treat. You shouldn't've touched my map.

TREAT. (*facing wall*) He should have warned you. (*PHILLIP grabs the torn pieces of the map and stuffs them into his pockets. He crosses to his jacket at the table and puts it on, moving to the closet. TREAT turns and sees him. PHILLIP takes a small satchel from the closet. He begins to shove the books and the shoe into it.*) I guess you don't need me anymore, then, Phillip, huh? I guess you can get along without me? (*PHILLIP is packing.*)

PHILLIP. (*on floor*) I'm gonna travel, Treat. I'm gonna visit places.

TREAT. I guess you don't need your big brother Treat no more.

PHILLIP. I'm gonna go wherever I wanna go. (*runs to window-seat, gets tape, comes back, tries to tape the map together*)

TREAT. Your big brother Treat who stole so we could have food on the table, so you could have them tuna fish sandwiches spread thick with Hellman's mayonnaise. And then when they came for you, your brother Treat who stood in the door blocking the way. Do you remember?

PHILLIP. I remember!

TREAT. You were crying. You hid in the closet.

PHILLIP. Yes!

TREAT. They tried to come in, but I stopped them. I bit the man's hand. I was only a little boy, but I bit his hand. Remember!

PHILLIP. I remember!

TREAT. They never bothered you again. I took care of you all these years, but you don't need me anymore. Is that right!

PHILLIP. I'm leaving! (*TREAT, stunned, moves back. He wanders around the room in a daze. PHILLIP on the floor is trying to put the map together. TREAT walks into the open closet. He pulls down the mother's coats. He crosses over to the coat that is on the floor. He drops to his knees and begins slamming it against the floor. He stops.*)

TREAT. Where was he all those years I was raising you. Where was he?

(*The front door opens. HAROLD stands there, his arm across the front of his jacket. PHILLIP looks up and notices him.*)

PHILLIP. I found my way home, Harold, only I got no more map.

HAROLD. (*at door*) It doesn't matter, Phillip. You can get a map at any gas station.

PHILLIP. I can.

HAROLD. All over America. You'll never be lost again.

PHILLIP. I'll never be lost. (*Pause. He picks up the pieces of the map.*) Maybe one day I won't even need a map.

HAROLD. Maybe. (*HAROLD closes the door. He crosses the room to his briefcase on the table. He has difficulty walking. He looks at the two of them, PHILLIP on the floor with the pieces of map, TREAT, on the floor, clinging to the coat.*) I have to go, boys.

PHILLIP. You're leaving?

HAROLD. I can't involve you anymore in this terrible business. I may get out of it myself. Look up that little widow lady, settle down, raise a family. (*HAROLD's coat comes open revealing a bloodstain from a gunshot. TREAT backs away. PHILLIP doesn't see it.*)

PHILLIP. Take me with you, Harold!

HAROLD. I can't do that, son. Don't worry, though, I'll always be with you.

PHILLIP. (*on floor*) You will.

HAROLD. Forever and ever. You can count on me. (*HAROLD crosses to the couch. He sits on the end. PHILLIP sees the wound.*)

PHILLIP. Harold!

HAROLD. (*on couch*) Fred had a nerve though, stole the German's key one night, big German son of a bitch . . . reached right into his pocket, stole his key. Never saw nothing like it, boy, orphans everywhere, hundreds of orphans running through the streets, pressing their faces against the windows . . . (*He has a pain.*) Big German son of a bitch beat the living hell out of us when we got back. We didn't mind, though. We seen what we had to see. (*another pain*)

PHILLIP. Harold!

HAROLD. You just needed a little encouragement, Phillip. (*looks over at TREAT*) How about you, son? (*reaches out his arm*) Come on over here. Let me give you some encouragement. (*TREAT doesn't move. HAROLD smiles at him.*) You're a Dead End Kid, ain't you? (*TREAT stares at him.*) I know a fucking Dead End Kid when I see one! (*HAROLD dies. A long pause.*)

PHILLIP. Harold? (*PHILLIP moves slowly to him. He touches him, tentatively. Quietly:*) Harold, please. (*He picks up his hand. He places it around his shoulder.*) Harold! I need some encouragement. (*PHILLIP begins to move HAROLD's arm back and forth across his shoulder, stroking himself with it. He is crying.*) Harold? (*TREAT has backed up into the open closet.*)

TREAT. He can't hear you, Phillip.

PHILLIP. (*stroking himself, slowly*) Harold?

TREAT. He's dead, Phillip. Can't you see? (*TREAT crosses to HAROLD and picks up his other hand. It is limp. He holds the hand, showing PHILLIP.*) He's dead. (*TREAT becomes aware of the hand in his own.*) I never touched his hand before. I never felt it. (*TREAT drops HAROLD's hand to the sofa.*)

PHILLIP. (*crying*) Harold? (*TREAT kneels down and picks up the hand again.*)

TREAT. (*to himself*) It's okay, though. He's dead. (*TREAT raises HAROLD's hand to his face. He presses the palm against his cheek. A long, long moment. He contorts his face and drops the hand again. He moves away.*) Something's wrong. Something hurts.

PHILLIP. What hurts? (*TREAT falls to his knees.*)

TREAT. (*on floor*) Inside me! Inside me! (*He is in

pain, a cry escapes from his lips.) NO! NO! NO! NO! (*trying to hold it back*) DON'T LEAVE ME! DON'T LEAVE ME, HAROLD! (*crawls over to HAROLD's body and holds him*) HAROLD! HAROLD! (*He is crying.*) I AM A DEAD END KID, HAROLD! I AM A FUCKING DEAD END KID! (*A terrible cry of pain. TREAT, sobbing, slumps to the foot of the couch. PHILLIP moves to him slowly. He grabs TREAT in a strong embrace. He struggles with TREAT for a moment holding him tightly. TREAT sobs like a baby in PHILLIP's comforting arms. PHILLIP cradles him.*)

CURTAIN

PRODUCTION NOTES

The play is open to various interpretations.

In the Los Angeles production, Phillip is not seen at the top of the play. Treat enters with his booty and Phillip comes slowly out of hiding.

At the top of Act One, Scene 3 in the New York production:

The next day. HAROLD tied up in the chair, tape covering his mouth. PHILLIP in the center of the room, wearing a football helmet and holding a child's size football, is calling a play. He fakes a hand-off to HAROLD, runs part-way across the room, throws the ball, and makes a diving catch on the floor by the window-seat. He gets up, sees something out the window, and jumps up on the window-seat.

The rest of the scene plays the same.

In the New York production at the top of the second act, music covers Phillip's discovery of the box with the yellow loafers. In the Los Angeles production, without music in the scene, we hear Harold, singing, off . . . "If I had the wings of an angel . . ." Phillip removes the loafer and says: "A shoe . . . only it's got no laces on it. It don't even got holes for laces. This must be the shoe Harold was talking about. This must be one of them magical loafers." He tries it on his foot but he can't squeeze it on. "Maybe there's some secret way it opens up, only I don't know the secret." Phillip notices Treat out the window. He runs upstairs with the loafers. The rest of the scene remains the same.

In Act One, Scene 2 when Harold is tied to the chair, his two feet should be tied together but not to the chair. This will give the actor leverage when he stands and hops across the room, the chair secured to his chest and back.

COSTUMES

ACT ONE

PHILLIP — torn sweatshirt over dirty T-shirt, ripped and filthy pajama bottoms, green high-topped sneakers w/ long laces untied

TREAT — army field jacket, plaid flannel shirt, jeans, sneakers

HAROLD — very sharp looking pin-striped 3-piece suit with tie in great disarray, alligator shoes — black

ACT TWO

PHILLIP — sweater vest, cotton shirt, slacks, green sneakers

Scene 3
Jacket, cap, yellow loafers

TREAT — sharp looking 3-piece "Pierre Cardin" suit, tie, silk shirt, brown alligator loafers

HAROLD — casual blue shirt, tie, black slacks, alligator shoes — black

Scene 3
Zippered jacket

PROPERTY LIST

The Set

US.R. a filthy, curtainless, closed window with one red shoe on the sill. On the openable window seat is a bottle of "bubble juice". To the left of the window a tilted wall sconce with one light bulb in its two holders, below it a wall switch and below this is a very small children's chair. Continuing toward S.L. a battered looking door with three small windows cut into it, a slide bolt lock, and, on the US. side of it, the address above the windows — 6040. To the left of the door is a stairway going up to the rest of the house, which disappears behind the U.C. wall. DS. of the newelled rail an end table which is decorated by a broken fan, an ashtray, a football helmet and small football.

On the U.C. wall is a Black Sabbath rock group poster and to its left about 4' of open space. Next to this a closet, inside of which are assorted shoes and a variety of women's coats. Next to the closet, a small alcove into which is set a small dresser, on top of which is a bunch of collected junk. Also in the alcove, a radiator, a broken vacuum cleaner, a broom with missing bristles and an overflowing garbage pail.

S.L. is a small pantry area with shelves filled with old food stuffs — flour & sugar cans, cereal boxes — and other assorted junk — old boots, a lawn sprinkler, etc. On top of the shelves to the right of another curtainless, dirty, closed window are enormous stacks of Star Kist tuna cans. To the right of the window are several paper plates encrusted with old tuna, a few plastic cups and a bottle of Early Times Bourbon, and an ashtray. Below the window is a long knit scarf.

A platform hugs the US.R. wall from below the window to the stairs. Just DS. of the platform is an old scrap of ugly green rug.

D.R. an old black and white television set with a long cord plugged into the wall S.R. of window. The TV is surrounded by old pillows and a dirty blanket. On top of the TV a stuffed bunny with both ears torn off and next to it a broken down Tonka truck.

C.S. is a couch covered by a torn and stained brown slip cover. On the couch is a Philadelphia Inquirer, two books, and, at either end, mismatched pillows. To the left of the couch an end table which is loaded with toy soldiers, broken crayons and an ashtray. DS. of the couch is a well-worn and dirty oriental carpet.

S.L. is a chipped, metal legged card table. On the table is a nearly empty jar of Hellmann's Real Mayonnaise with a tablespoon in it, and a plastic ashtray. Around the table are three mismatched chairs — all various types and old but which must be sturdy. Hanging above the table a black cast iron chandelier w/4 candle bulbs. At extreme S.L. is another wall with a doorway to the kitchen. Of the kitchen only two loudly wall-papered walls and a wicker decoration piece are seen when the door is opened.

Along the downstage edge of the stage, and scattered throughout the floor area, are stacks and piles of assorted garbage torn and ragged piles of Philadelphia Inquirers, dirty tuna dishes, toys, a record player, spoons, etc.

At intermission the room has changed:

Sheer curtains are hung in both windows. The wall sconce is straightened and in place of the one household bulb is placed two fancy candle-like bulbs. The S.R. end table is cleared and a lava lamp placed on top of it. On the wall at the foot of the stairs a framed painting — something abstract and inexpensive looking — is hung.

The Black Sabbath poster is removed and in its place goes a Philadelphia Orchestra poster featuring Ricardo Muti. Against the wall U.C. is a well-stocked liquor cart w/plenty of Bourbon, glasses, ice bucket & water pitcher.

The alcove is cleared out of the vacuum cleaner and broom. The dresser is cleared and a kitschy plaster imitation Greek statuette replaces the junk. The shelves of the pantry are cleared and refilled with crystal glasses, vases and better quality food. The tuna cans are replaced by a stainless-steel coffee pot. The plates, cups, and liquor bottle are cleared but the scarf remains. US. of the kitchen door is a rubber coated wire rack of food packages — noodles, Rice-a-roni, Ovaltine, bread crumbs, etc.

The ugly green rug in front of the door is removed to reveal a handsome Persian rug and the main rug in front of the couch is covered by a plush salmon carpet. The couch cover is removed to expose a couch with a pretty floral pattern. The pillows & blanket in front of the TV are eliminated in favor of multicoloured new pillows, but the bunny remains. The S.L. end table is cleared and the toy soldiers replaced by an artificial flower arrangement in a crystal vase and a glass ashtray.

The papers, garbage, plates and toys are removed.

The S.L. table area is re-done with a new octagonal table with table cloth, 3 placemats, and a white glass ashtray, shaped like a butterfly which contains a ½ smoked Tiparillo. The chairs around it are now matching, white, & cushioned.

Hand Props

by scene break-down, placement, character

Act I, Scene 1

o.l. kitchen
TREAT—Hershey's chocolate milk—Qt.

o.r. dressing room
TREAT—assorted jewelry—chains, bracelet, 1 man's watch, one woman's watch with small band, three wallets filled with cash and credit cards and extra loose cash, switchblade with 7½″ blade, bubble gum, spray water bottle (for "sweat")

Couch
PHILLIP—two books w/words underlined, Philadelphia Inquirer with 2nd section words underlined

s.l. table
PHILLIP—jar of nearly empty Hellmann's mayonnaise with tablespoon

s.r. window sill
PHILLIP—red shoe, high heeled

Window seat
PHILLIP—"bubble juice"

At top of stairs
PHILLIP—Hydrogen Peroxide bottle, cup of blood w/Q-tip, crash box

Act I, Scene 2

Pantry
PHILLIP—long knit scarf
TREAT—stacks of tuna

o.l. kitchen
PHILLIP—crash supplies (pots, pans, tins), 48′ of cloth rope

In S.L. end table
　PHILLIP — 8' cloth rope

O.R. dressing room
　HAROLD — handkerchief, briefcase w/folios filled
　　w/stocks & bonds, bar glass
　TREAT — switchblade

S.R. in window seat
　TREAT — red shoe, masking tape w/double stick tape

Act I, Scene 3

Pantry
　PHILLIP — long knit scarf
　HAROLD — bottle of Early Times, ashtray

At top of stairs
　HAROLD — Tiparillos & silver lighter, lint brush
　　(used off), snub-nosed revolver, little black book,
　　8 $1000 bills

S.R. end table
　PHILLIP — small football, football helmet

Personal
　TREAT — switchblade

S.R. table
　HAROLD — ashtray

Act II, Scene 1

O.R. dressing room
　TREAT — sunglasses, large bottle Hellmann's mayon-
　　naise in brown paper bag, Chicago Tribune, Amer-
　　ican Express card, Tiparillos & fancy lighter

U.C. liquor cart
　Bourbon, glasses, ice, water pitcher

Couch
> PHILLIP — gift wrapped shoe box w/yellow loafers, shoe-horn & "magic ribbon"

O.L.
> HAROLD — Tiparillos, lighter

Act II, Scene 2

O.L. kitchen
> HAROLD — Tiparillos, map of Philadelphia, gold pen
> PHILLIP — soup bowl w/lobster claw, spoon, soup, 2 napkins

O.R.
> TREAT — 45 semiautomatic in shoulder holster, briefcase w/folios, spray bottle (for sweat)

Act II, Scene 3

Couch
> TREAT — 5 books w/underlined words under cushion, high heeled red shoe under cushion

On stage
> Liquor cart

Closet
> TREAT — big furry brown coat

O.L.
> TREAT — spray bottle, switchblade
> HAROLD — Phillip's hat & coat, Harold's jacket

Act II, Scene 4

On stage
> TREAT—big furry brown coat, liquor cart w/Bourbon & water pitcher
> PHILLIP—book bag on shelf in closet

O.L. kitchen
> PHILLIP—empty jar of Hellmann's

O.R.
> PHILLIP—bunch of flowers, subway token, map of Philadelphia
> HAROLD—blood in squeeze bottle, bloody clothes— shirt, jacket, pants, spray bottle

Couch
> TREAT—5 books w/underlined words, high heeled red shoe

Closet
> TREAT—assorted women's coats

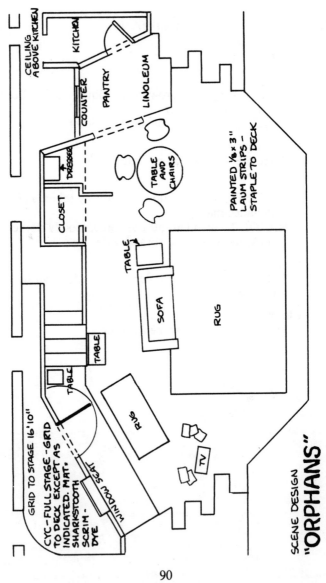

SCENE DESIGN
"ORPHANS"

90

Other Publications for Your Interest

THE CURATE SHAKESPEARE AS YOU LIKE IT
(LITTLE THEATRE—COMEDY)

By DON NIGRO

4 men, 3 women—Bare stage

This extremely unusual and original piece is subtitled: "The record of one company's attempt to perform the play by William Shakespeare". When the very prolific Mr. Nigro was asked by a professional theatre company to adapt *As You Like It* so that it could be performed by a company of seven he, of course, came up with a completely original play about a rag-tag group of players comprised of only seven actors led by a dotty old curate who nonetheless must present Shakespeare's play; and the dramatic interest, as well as the comedy, is in their hilarious attempts to impersonate all of Shakespeare's multitude of characters. The play has had numerous productions nationwide, all of which have come about through word of mouth. We are very pleased to make this "underground comic classic" widely available to theatre groups who like their comedy wide open and theatrical. (#5742)

SEASCAPE WITH SHARKS AND DANCER
(LITTLE THEATRE—DRAMA)

By DON NIGRO

1 man, 1 woman—Interior

This is a fine new play by an author of great talent and promise. We are very glad to be introducing Mr. Nigro's work to a wide audience with *Seascape With Sharks and Dancer*, which comes directly from a sold-out, critically acclaimed production at the world-famous Oregon Shakespeare Festival. The play is set in a beach bungalow. The young man who lives there has pulled a lost young woman from the ocean. Soon, she finds herself trapped in his life and torn between her need to come to rest somewhere and her certainty that all human relationships turn eventually into nightmares. The struggle between his tolerant and gently ironic approach to life and her strategy of suspicion and attack becomes a kind of war about love and creation which neither can afford to lose. In other words, this is quite an offbeat, wonderful love story We would like to point out that the play also contains a wealth of excellent **monologue** and **scene material.** (#21060)

Other Publications for Your Interest

HUSBANDRY
(LITTLE THEATRE—DRAMA)

By PATRICK TOVATT

2 men, 2 women—Interior

At its recent world premiere at the famed Actors Theatre of Louisville, this enticing new drama moved an audience of theatre professionals up off their seats and on to their feet to cheer. Mr. Tovatt has given us an insightful drama about what is happening to the small, family farm in America—and what this means for the future of the country. The scene is a farmhouse whose owners are on the verge of losing their farm. They are visited by their son and his wife, who live "only" eight hours' drive away. The son has a good job in the city, and his wife does, too. The son, Harry, is really put on the horns of a dilemma when he realizes that he is his folks' only hope. The old man can't go it alone anymore—and he needs his son. Pulling at him from the other side is his wife, who does not want to leave her job and uproot her family to become a farm wife. *Husbandry,* then, is ultimately about what it means to be a *husband*—both in the farm and in the family sense. *Variety* praised the "delicacy of Tovatt's dialogue", and called the play "a literate exploration of family responsibilities in a mobile society." Said *Time*: "The play simmers so gently for so long, as each potential confrontation is deflected with Chekhovian shrugs and silences, that when it boils into hostility it sears the audience."   (#10169)

CLARA'S PLAY
(LITTLE THEATRE—DRAMA)

By JOHN OLIVE

3 men, 1 woman—Exterior

Clara, an aging spinster, lives alone in a remote farmhouse. She is the last surviving member of one of the area's most prominent families. It is summer, 1915. Enter an immigrant, feisty soul named Sverre looking for a few days' work before moving on. But Clara's farm needs more than just a few days' work, and Sverre stays on to help Clara fix up and run the farm. It soon becomes clear unscrupulous local businessmen are bilking Clara out of money and hope to gain control of her property. Sverre agrees to stay on to help Clara keep her family's property. "A story of determination, loyalty. It has more than a measure of love, of resignation, of humor and loyalty."—Chicago Sun-Times. "A playwright of unusual sensitivity in delineating character and exploring human relationships." —Chicago Tribune. "Gracefully-written, with a real sense of place."—Village Voice. A recent success both at Chicago's fine Wisdom Bridge Theatre and at the Great American Play Festival of the world-reknowned Actors Theatre of Louisville; and, on tour, starring Jean Stapleton.   (#5076)

Other Publications for Your Interest

A WEEKEND NEAR MADISON
(LITTLE THEATRE—COMIC DRAMA)
By KATHLEEN TOLAN

2 men, 3 women—Interior

This recent hit from the famed Actors Theatre of Louisville, a terrific ensemble play about male-female relationships in the 80's, was praised by *Newsweek* as "warm, vital, glowing . . . full of wise ironies and unsentimental hopes". The story concerns a weekend reunion of old college friends now in their early thirties. The occasion is the visit of Vanessa, the queen bee of the group, who is now the leader of a lesbian/feminist rock band. Vanessa arrives at the home of an old friend who is now a psychiatrist hand in hand with her naif-like lover, who also plays in the band. Also on hand are the psychiatrist's wife, a novelist suffering from writer's block; and his brother, who was once Vanessa's lover and who still loves her. In the course of the weekend, Vanessa reveals that she and her lover desperately want to have a child—and she tries to persuade her former male lover to father it, not understanding that he might have some feelings about the whole thing. *Time Magazine* heard "the unmistakable cry of an infant hit . . . Playwright Tolan's work radiates promise and achievement."
(#25051)

PASTORALE
(LITTLE THEATRE—COMEDY)
By DEBORAH EISENBERG

3 men, 4 women—Interior
(plus 1 or 2 bit parts and 3 optional extras)

"Deborah Eisenberg is one of the freshest and funniest voices in some seasons."—Newsweek. Somewhere out in the country Melanie has rented a house and in the living room she, her friend Rachel who came for a weekend but forgets to leave, and their school friend Steve (all in their mid-20s) spend nearly a year meandering through a mental landscape including such concerns as phobias, friendship, work, sex, slovenliness and epistemology. Other people happen by: Steve's young girlfriend Celia, the virtuous and annoying Edie, a man who Melanie has picked up in a bar, and a couple who appear during an intense conversation and observe the sofa is on fire. The lives of the three friends inevitably proceed and eventually draw them, the better prepared perhaps by their months on the sofa, in separate directions. "The most original, funniest new comic voice to be heard in New York theater since Beth Henley's 'Crimes of the Heart.'"—N.Y. Times. "A very funny, stylish comedy."—The New Yorker. "Wacky charm and wayward wit."—New York Magazine. "Delightful."—N.Y. Post. "Uproarious . . . the play is a world unto itself, and it spins."—N.Y. Sunday Times.
(#18016)

Other Publications for Your Interest

TALKING WITH . . .
(LITTLE THEATRE)

By JANE MARTIN

11 women—Bare stage

Here, at last, is the collection of eleven extraordinary monologues for eleven actresses which had them on their feet cheering at the famed Actors Theatre of Louisville—audiences, critics and, yes, even jaded theatre professionals. The mysteriously pseudonymous Jane Martin is truly a "find", a new writer with a wonderfully idiosyncratic style, whose characters alternately amuse, move and frighten us always, however, speaking to us from the depths of their souls. The characters include a baton twirler who has found God through twirling; a fundamentalist snake handler, an ex-rodeo rider crowded out of the life she has cherished by men in 3-piece suits who want her to dress up "like Minnie damn Mouse in a tutu"; an actress willing to go to any length to get a job; and an old woman who claims she once saw a man with "cerebral walrus" walk into a McDonald's and be healed by a Big Mac. "Eleven female monologues, of which half a dozen verge on brilliance."—London Guardian. "Whoever (Jane Martin) is, she's a writer with an original imagination."—Village Voice. "With Jane Martin, the monologue has taken on a new poetic form, intensive in its method and revelatory in its impact."—Philadelphia Inquirer. "A dramatist with an original voice . . . (these are) tales about enthusiasms that become obsessions, eccentric confessionals that levitate with religious symbolism and gladsome humor."—N.Y. Times. *Talking With . . .* is the 1982 winner of the American Theatre Critics Association Award for Best Regional Play. (#22009)

HAROLD AND MAUDE
(ADVANCED GROUPS—COMEDY)

By COLIN HIGGINS

9 men, 8 women—Various settings

Yes: *the* Harold and Maude! This is a stage adaptation of the wonderful movie about the suicidal 19 year-old boy who finally learns how to truly *live* when he meets up with that delightfully whacky octogenarian, Maude. Harold is the proverbial Poor Little Rich Kid. His alienation has caused him to attempt suicide several times, though these attempts are more cries for attention than actual attempts. His peculiar attachment to Maude, whom he meets at a funeral (a mutual passion), is what saves him—and what captivates us. This new stage version, a hit in France directed by the internationally-renowned Jean-Louis Barrault, will certainly delight both afficionados of the film and new-comers to the story. "Offbeat upbeat comedy."—Christian Science Monitor. (#10032)

Other Publications for Your Interest

SEA MARKS

(LITTLE THEATRE—DRAMA)

By GARDNER McKAY

1 woman, 1 man—Unit set

Winner of L.A. Drama Critics Circle Award "Best Play." This is the "funny, touching, bit-tersweet tale" (Sharbutt, A.P.) of a fisherman living on a remote island to the west of Ireland who has fallen in love with, in retrospect, a woman he's glimpsed only once. Unschooled in letter-writing, he tries his utmost to court by mail and, after a year-and-a-half, succeeds in arranging a rendezvous at which, to his surprise, she persuades him to live with her in Liverpool. Their love affair ends only when he is forced to return to the life he better understands. "A masterpiece." (The Tribune, Worcester, Mass.) "Utterly winning," (John Simon, New York Magazine.) "There's abundant humor, surprisingly honest humor, that grows between two impossible partners. The reaching out and the fearful withdrawal of two people who love each other but whose lives simply cannot be fused: a stubborn, decent, attractive and touching collision of temperments, honest in por-traiture and direct in speech. High marks for SEA MARKS!" (Walter Kerr, New York Times.) "Fresh as a May morning. A lovely, tender and happily humorous love story." (Elliot Norton, Boston Herald American.) "It could easily last forever in actors' classrooms and audition studios." (Oliver, The New Yorker)

THE WOOLGATHERER

(LITTLE THEATRE—DRAMA)

By WILLIAM MASTROSIMONE

1 man, 1 woman—Interior

In a dreary Philadelphia apartment lives Rose, a shy and slightly creepy five-and-dime salesgirl. Into her life saunters Cliff, a hard-working, hard-drinking truck driver—who has picked up Rose and been invited back to her room. Rose is an innocent whose whole life centers around reveries and daydreams. He is rough and witty—but it's soon apparent—just as starved for love as she is. This little gem of a play was a recent success at New York's famed Circle Repertory starring Peter Weller and Patricia Wettig. Actors take note: The Woolgatherer has several excellent monologues. ". . . energy, compassion and theatrical sense are there."—N.Y. Times. ". . . another emotionally wrenching experience no theatre enthusiast should miss."—Rex Reed. "Mastrosimone writes consistently witty and sometimes lyrical dialogue."—New York Magazine. "(Mastrosimone) has a knack for composing wildly humorous lines at the same time that he is able to penetrate people's hearts and dreams."—Hollywood Reporter.

Other Publications for Your Interest

MAGIC TIME
(LITTLE THEATRE—COMEDY)

By JAMES SHERMAN

5 men, 3 women—Interior

Off Broadway audiences and the critics enjoyed and praised this engaging backstage comedy about a troupe of professional actors (non-Equity) preparing to give their last performance of the summer in *Hamlet*. Very cleverly the backstage relationships mirror the onstage ones. For instance, Larry Mandell (Laertes) very much resents the performance of David Singer (Hamlet), as he feels *he* should have had the role. Also, he is secretly in love with Laurie Black (Ophelia)—who is living with David. David, meanwhile, is holding a mirror up to nature, but not to himself—and Laurie is trying to get him to be honest with her about his feelings. There's also a Horatio who has a thriving career in TV commercials; a Polonius who gave up acting to have a family and teach high school, but who has decidedly second thoughts, and a Gertrude and Claudius who are married in *real* life. This engaging play is an absolute *must* for all non-Equity groups, such as colleges, community theatres, and non-Equity pros or semi-pros. "There is an artful innocence in 'Magic Time' . . . It is also delightful."—N.Y. Times. ". . . captivating little backstage comedy . . . it is entirely winning . . . boasts one of the most entertaining band of Shakespearean players I've run across."—N.Y. Daily News. (#15028)

BADGERS
(LITTLE THEATRE—COMEDY)

By DONALD WOLLNER

6 men, 2 women—Interior, w/insert

"'Badgers! . . . opened the season at the Manhattan Punchline while Simon and Garfunkel were offering a concert in Central Park. In tandem, the two events were a kind of déjà vu for the 60's, when all things seemed possible, even revolution. As we watch 'Badgers' we can hear a subliminal 'Sounds of Silence'."—N.Y. Times. The time is 1967. The place is the University of Wisconsin during the Dow Chemical sit-in/riots. This cross-section of college campus life in that turbulent decade focuses on the effect of the events on the characters: "Wollner's amiable remembrance adds up to a sort of campus roll-call—here are radicalized kids from Eastern high schools, 'WASP' accountancy majors who didn't make Harvard or Penn. Most significant is the playwright's contention that none were touched lightly by those times . . . he has a strong sense of the canvas he's drawing on."—Soho Weekly News. If you loved *Moonchildren,* you're certain to love this "wry and gentle look at a toubled time" (Bergen Record). (#3998)